GENE KEMP

Charlie Lewis Plays
for Time

illustrated by
Vanessa Julian-Ottie

faber and faber

First published in 1984
Reset and published in this paperback edition in 2000
by Faber and Faber Limited
3 Queen Square, London WCIN 3AU

Photoset by Avon DataSet Ltd, Bidford on Avon
Printed in England by Mackays of Chatham plc, Chatham, Kent

A CIP record for this book
is available from the British Library

ISBN 0–571–20650–6

2 4 6 8 10 9 7 5 3 1

Gene Kemp's first books, a series of stories about an amazing pig called Tamworth, immediately established her as one of the funniest and most imaginative authors writing for children. ~~~~ ~~~~ wrote *The Turbulent Term of Tyke Tiler*, a grou~~~~ break~~~~g school story which won th~~~~ ~~~~ibrary Assoc~~~~ion's C~~~~negie Medal and shot to the ~~~~ ~~~~f the child~~~~n's bestse~~~~ ~~~~ ~~~~ther titles set in ~~~~cklepit Combined S~~~~ool followed, along w~~~~ ~~~~lecti~~~~ ~~~~f short stories, novels for teenagers, fiction for younger ~~~~dren and a powerful narrative poem, *The Mink War*. *Cha~~~~e Lewis Plays for Time* was runner up in the Whitbread Awa~~~~. She is now recognized as one of the most popular contem~~~~orary children's authors, and she was awarded an honorary degree in 1984 in recognition of her achievement as a writer. She lives in Exeter, Devon.

by the same author

BLUEBEARD'S CASTLE
THE ROOM WITH NO WINDOWS
ROUNDABOUT
TAMWORTH PIG RIDES AGAIN
THE TYKE TILER JOKE BOOK

edited by Gene Kemp

REBEL REBEL

for Allan Fouracre

'There is a limit – one finds it by experience, Beetle – beyond which it is never safe to pursue private vendettas, because – don't move – sooner or later one comes – into collision with the – higher authority, who has studied the animal.'

Stalky & Co. RUDYARD KIPLING

CUT EDUCATION COSTS!
Shoot the teachers.

Characters in the Story

At Nos. 6 and 8, Rolleston Crescent, Redmount, ISCA
IS89 67DS

No 6	*No 8*
Mr Moffat (unemployed)	Marian Forrest (concert pianist)
Mrs Moffat (cleaner)	Dorothy Clyde (her manager/secretary)
Charles Moffat (Chas, dealer in old bikes)	Hortense Vandenburgh (*au pair*/minder)
Tarquin Moffat (unemployed)	
Kevin Moffat (at the Dawson Comprehensive)	Charlie Lewis
Patricia Moffat	
Rodney Moffat	
Bernadette Moffat	All at Cricklepit
Duwayne Moffat	Combined –
Gary Moffat	
Toyah Moffat	

Also

Mrs William Merchant (Bonfire)
Mr Walter Schliemann (Professor of Music: London)
Bus driver
Guide

I

Put a drawing pin on your teacher's chair.
That will keep him on his toes.

And Rocket's head smacked into the bean bag, which couldn't hurt Rocket but proved just too much for the bean bag. It burst, shooting hard pinky brown beans all over the hall, popcorn in a fry pan, over benches, through wall bars, on to the trampoline, above the ropes, pinging against windows, an indoor hailstorm.

'Smashing,' yelled Rocket, gone mad with delight.

'Enough is enough,' cried Mr Merchant, Sir. 'That's it. Finish. Time to go home, thank goodness. Clear up now. Everything in place. Trish, you organize the beans. What a mess.'

'Well, Sir, you said we could pelt you with bean bags on the last day of term.'

'I did? I must have been crazy. Right, as soon as everything's sorted get back to the classroom for the end of the day and the end of term.'

Later, back in the hall we sang, 'At Easter time the lilies fair and lovely flowers bloom everywhere, At Easter time, At Easter time, How glad . . .,' Rocket whooping up and down like a distressed whale.

'Tell him to shut up,' I hissed at Trish, his twin. Without lifting her eyes from her hymn book, she kicked him on the

shin and dug him with her elbow. And Rocket shut up. But his face darkened and fell sad, a cloud crossing the sun, and I felt mean, why did I have to interfere? For really, to me, his singing wasn't that much worse than old Champers, our music teacher, bashing and crashing away on the piano, two bars ahead of us as usual, and nobody said that was grisly – which it was. But I was always scared that one day somebody was going to splatter Rocket when he made that mind-boggling din, probably me.

Back in the classroom once more we said goodbye to Sir, Trish wrapped like a python round his middle. She's got a crush on him.

'Have a good holiday, everyone. Enjoy yourselves.'

'You doing anything special, Sir?'

'Working on a plan to introduce cannibalism into schools. Get the real in-depth feeling of exploring the unknown that way.'

'You're having us on, Sir.'

'My, you're quick, Brian.'

'Hear you're gonna be a Dad this Easter.'

'That's right but not till afterwards actually.'

'D'you want a girl or a boy?'

'We don't mind as long as it's healthy and normal.'

'That'll take a bit of doing, Sir.'

'And what do you mean by that, Trish Moffat?'

'With you for a Dad, Sir? Anything's possible.'

'Lucky for you lot it's the end of term, or it would be severe torture for that remark.'

Trish sighed, 'Roll on next term,' so I peeled her off Sir before she got too sloppy, then we set off after Rocket before he could encounter one of his own special disasters.

2

We all wait for Trish to come up with ideas, set alight by her hair, the colour of red poppies. Most of the Moffats have white hair, Gary and Duwayne, the little kids, and two older ones, Kev at the Comprehensive and Tark on the dole. They're all as thick as short planks, Trish says, but not Chas, who's eighteen, with a black Mohican and five old bikes. Trish thinks a lot of Chas. Then there's the Cool Cat, Bernadette, in the third year at school, just below ours. Her hair is nearer silver and she sings like a bird out of the sky. And the littlest one, Toyah, with orange hair this time, who's screaming murder on two legs, which she hasn't been on very long being about two and a bit. I take care never to be left alone with Toyah. She might want to colour me green or stick a pin in me and see if I scream. Then, of course, there's Rocket, also with white hair, and mad. They're all crazy, yes, but Rocket is something else, unique, gone beyond, the flip side of Trish, his twin. And there's not one item of resemblance between them (except they both belong to the human race, though even that's doubtful in Rocket's case), which just goes to prove something, though I'm not sure what. Different eggs, says Trish if you ask her why.

The Moffats live next door to me in a big tall house, the twin of ours, and without them life would just be school and

4

music lessons. For my mother is away a lot, being a concert pianist, and my father is away all the time, in fact I'm not sure I'd know him if I met him, he's been gone so long, and we don't have photographs in our house, which is clean and tidy and organized and beautiful, people say. And also absolutely dead boring, except for all the musical instruments, records etc., so I spend as much time as I can at the Moffats, where the house is always full of people having rows, and the garden's a jungle with wild animals (us) and traps (old bikes, prams, fridges, holes and huts) – great. They've also got an enormous TV. We don't have one because it might stop me doing my practice. We don't have pop records either but I deal with *that*.

We'd been at home a fortnight and it had begun to drag a bit. We sat on boxes, one morning, at the bottom of the jungle where Hortense couldn't get at me because of the Great Nettle Barrier. Hortense is from Belgium and is supposed to look after me, and she's rotten at it, but we don't let on, as she wants to keep the job, because she's got a boy-friend here, and I have this feeling that a really good minder might stop me spending so much time at the Moffats. Her English is lousy, and my French is worse, so we don't talk much. All she ever says is, ' 'ave you done your practeese?' and, 'Zose naughtee cheeldren cannot come een 'ere.' That's the Moffats.

'What we gonna do, Trish? It's a bit boring.'

'I wanted to play cricket again, but Rocket would lose the ball.'

Rocket was swinging up and down on a tree rope, shrieking, 'Me Tarzan, walloolloolloo,' a horrible sight and a horrible noise, even worse than his hymn singing. He also thinks he can fly.

'Let's go down to the river.'

'No, it's spoilt since they cleaned it up to stop it flooding. Might as well be an old people's park.'

'Let's go down the valley and have a picnic. Might get some tadpoles. Or some fish.'

Trish's eyes were swivelling towards her nose as they do when she gets pleased about something. Sometimes it can mean we're heading for trouble. She's got these huge brown eyes with thick black lashes, and at one time she wouldn't even wear her glasses, which she hated. Specs are for other people, not me, she'd say and she threw one pair in the pond and the next in the Great Nettle Barrier, though Rocket found them by setting fire to it, not that the specs were much good by then, and after a bit, the Great Nettle Barrier grew even higher. But then Mr Merchant asked if she wanted to be known as Professor or Squinter. She thought about this and has worn them ever since.

'Charlie, can you get us some grub? Some of your fancy stuff would be nice. I liked that c-c-caviare you sneaked out.'

'Yeah, I'll get some.'

'What have we got?'

'Not much,' Rocket said, coming down from the tree. 'I've already looked. Tark 'ad 'is rotten mates in last night, playing records, and they've cleaned us out.'

'We'll buy some, then. Cough up, everybody. Chas gave me a pound for fixin' his cassette player, so I'll lob in fifty p.,' said Trish.

'Charlie's got money,' said Bernadette. 'Loads of it.' Of all the Moffats it's Bernadette who hates me. I never know what I've done.

'Right. I'll get some food and some money, then we can call in at the shop on the way there.'

'We all put in something, not just Charlie and me,' Trish said. 'No, not you, Toyah. Everybody else.'

Rocket had fished around in his jeans and come up with fourpence.

'Hey, what's it like to be rich, Charlie?' he asked.

'How the heck would I know?'

'You've always got money.'

'My mother just gives me some when she goes away, that's all.'

'I wish it was my all,' Bernadette sniffed. 'You've got it easy, Charlie.'

'Oh, let's get going,' Trish sang out. So we did.

We set off, Toyah perched on blankets in the old pram pushed by Bernadette. On the way we stopped at the corner shop kept by Malcolm, a walk-round-help-yourself one.

'Out,' he said, as we crowded in, 'except for you, you, and you,' Trish, Bernadette and me, but Toyah started to yell her head off so Bernadette went out to her. Toyah's almost the only person she seems fond of. When we'd chosen our food we set off, piling carriers and cartons and cans into the pram, and warned Toyah not to touch it.

The valley sides are steep and it wasn't easy getting the pram and Toyah down to the stream. Bernadette gave Toyah a ride on her back, and Rocket and I carted down the pram, directed by Trish. And at last we settled under the trees just beginning to come out into leaf, and where one had recently fallen across the stream making a leafy bridge, a very pretty spot it was, with boulders, and lots of moss and flowers. We took out the first bag of food.

'We'll divide it up fairly. No, you're not starting with that lolly, Toyah . . .'

'Gary is!'

'Look out . . .' yelled Duwayne.

7

'Oh no,' cried Bernadette, looking up. So did we all. And we were surrounded by a whole lot of cows, who had arrived from nowhere, quietly munching, and formed a half circle round us, the stream behind.

'Take no notice,' bellowed Trish. 'They're harmless.'

But she was wasting her time, for we all got up, grabbing food, Bernadette grabbing Toyah.

'I'll send them off,' shouted Rocket, waving his arms like a windmill in a hurricane, and leapt at them. What they thought of this I don't know but one of them lifted up its head and snorted, stamping its hoof in the mud churned up by their hooves.

That did it. Except for Trish there was a mad rush for the tree bridge, Duwayne leading the way, Bernadette clutching Toyah, me bringing up the rear with Rocket, both of us trying to get the pram, and our food, over to the other side. It was still covered with branches and April buds, and as we heaved it along, the pram jammed, Rocket tugged, I tugged, and it wobbled dangerously.

'Look out! Hang on to it!' I yelled, trying to do just that, but Rocket shoved it wildly over a lumpy joint, and between the pair of us, the pram slowly, slowly, slowly toppled over into the stream, a fair way below, for its banks are as steep as

8

the valley sides. Down went all the food into the mud, and the blanket and various comics followed and settled down over it as we all gazed.

Trish was dancing up and down and yelling on the other side of the stream.

'You stupid, half-witted idiots! Look what you've done! All that lovely grub. How could you? And the cows are going, anyway.'

Yes, they were. Having wrecked our outing they turned their dirty rear ends on us and were heading east or west or someplace else.

'I'll save the grub,' yelled Rocket.

'No, don't do it,' shrieked Trish. Too late, with a gigantic splash, soaking us as well, Rocket did his famous flying jump into the stream. Not that it mattered, for almost immediately it started to pour with rain, mixed with hailstones. As we trailed home Rocket was no wetter than the rest of us.

Mrs Moffat's cleaning job begins at five in the morning and stops at one. We had timed coming back nicely to arrive with her. She went on for ages. I know where Trish gets it from.

I ducked out of it and headed for home, music and peace. It's great to be out with the Moffats and great to get back to the music afterwards. I crept into the kitchen and dried myself off, and made a hot drink. Hortense didn't seem to be about. Two seconds later there came a tap at the door to a rhythm I worked out long ago. It was Trish and Rocket.

'Is it safe to come in? Mum's in a mood and Tark and Chas are fighting over a girl.'

'Yes. She's out, I think. Come up to my room and we'll listen to some records. I've got a new album. Don't break anything, Rocket, for Pete's sake.'

9

Trish is allowed in sometimes but never Rocket, ever since they found him sliding up and down my mother's Bechstein, with a broken vase lying on the floor. Didn't look much to me, but they said it was Chinese. Hortense had hysterics, cos Dorothy nearly gave her the push over that one, so now she's very fierce with him.

'I don't want to listen to a record, Charlie. I want to have a bath. I love your bathroom. It's like the Arabian Nights.'

'You must be nuts having a bath when you don't have to. Clean it up, so she won't know.'

'I always do.'

In my room I got out my new album from my secret rock and pop collection that only Trish and Rocket know about, and we listened with headphones on, so if Hortense found us she wouldn't know what we were listening to. She did put her head round the door, but I'd heard her come in and shoved Rocket in the wardrobe. She said she'd be in the kitchen. Then Trish came in reeking of bath oil, the sort that makes wonderful things happen, that's a laugh, so I said she must sneak Rocket out of the front door, so Hortense wouldn't see him or smell her.

'You're so secretive and sly, Charlie. One day, you'll find yourself doing something even you don't know about.'

'I can't follow that. See you at school, tomorrow.'

'An' I'll see Sir. Oh, great. I'm glad the holidays are over.'

'I'm not,' said Rocket. 'Me an' school don't get on much.'

After they'd gone, I tried to capture a tune that was there about the stream and the grub – oh, I was hungry – I'd only had time for a bag of crisps, I'd go down and get something in a minute. Just that tune, pretty, the sound of the stream tumbling down a tiny waterfall, the birds singing, the buds, but it kept changing into something sinister and stormish, I couldn't stop it. Perhaps it was the thunder and hail outside. I shivered, suddenly, as if I had to go out into the storm or into a dark tunnel. Yuck, I needed grub, that's all.

3

Poor old teacher. We missed you so
When into hospital you did go.
For you to remain would be a sin,
We're sorry about the banana skin.

On the way to school Trish talked about being in the cricket team. Last year she'd been twelfth man, I mean person, she said, and she was sure she'd be chosen this year. Mr Merchant almost promised, she went on, but I didn't listen much for I'd just looked round.

'Rocket's hopped it.'

'Oh, hell's bells, he would.'

'Do you think we ought to go after him?'

'Mum said to keep an eye on him, see that he got to school in one piece. But you'd think he could look after himself by now. He's the same age as me.'

'No one would think so. I thought twins were supposed to be identical and all that. No one could be more different to look at than you two. I certainly can't see you and Rocket deceiving the entire school by pretending to be each other, like in books.'

'No, sad. It would be great if we could, whereas all that really happens is I have to look after him.'

'He's been much better lately. He'll be OK.'

'Yeh, he'll get to school all right. Come on, Charlie, I can't wait to see Sir. I've got a new joke for him.'

'Not that corny one about being teacher's pet because he can't afford a dog? Boring. Boring.'

'You know a better one?'

'No, I can't remember jokes.'

'Then keep your big mouth shut, Charlie Lewis.'

So we started to race each other and arrived at school out of breath, stamping and steaming. We dumped our anoraks and bags in the cloakroom, which had to be the same as last term, and the thought jumped up suddenly in my mind that next term was . . .

'Charlie, it's the last time . . . the last term . . . next term we shall be somewhere else,' wailed Trish, eyes swivelling wildly and heading for her nose. 'You'll be all posh at that boarding school and I'll be at the Comprehensive. Oh, Charlie, I don't want to leave Sir . . .' and enormous tears started to spurt.

'You're not chatting up a girl, Charlie Lewis, are you?' sneered a voice belonging to Brian Cooper, a pain in the neck if ever there was one. At school it was difficult to be friendly with Trish, for you always got tormented. But Trish was ready to fight back. She always is.

'You are a sexist pig, Brian Cooper. And you know what Sir has to say about that sort of thing. We're not having it in this school. Come on, Charlie.'

'You go on. I'm not quite ready yet.'

'Charlie Lewis, you're scared, chicken, a coward. You always were.'

'I just like a quiet life. Besides, I ought to see if Rocket's around yet.'

'I'm off to see Sir. I'm gonna creep up behind him and then spring on him.'

'You're fantasizing. You wouldn't dare.'

'Bets?'

'OK, I'm coming. This I must see.' And I followed her into the classroom even if Brian was singing lovey, dovey, doo behind us.

But Trish didn't creep up behind Sir and spring on him, for there in the classroom, standing by the teacher's desk which just about came up to his knees, stood a man, tall and straight, wearing a dark blazer and a tie with crests on it.

He stared at us and Trish threw her plait which she wears at school over her shoulder just as I'd opened my mouth to speak and it went in, hairy and ticklish, so I choked while some joker behind thumped me hard on my back, saying, 'Choke up chicken,' and nearly smashing me to the floor which is all you need, and I could feel my face turning as red as Trish's hair. Somehow I reached the table where I sit with Trish and Rocket, Julia Wenham, Alex from Jamaica and Tam Lann, a Vietnamese boat boy, and the brightest in the class though he couldn't speak any English when he came about a year ago. Rocket sits next to Trish so that she can keep him under control, after he's been programmed on what he's got to do that day by Sir.

'And I get fed up. Why don't you just tie him down and give me a break?' she asked one day, so Sir moved Rocket to another table. In the week that followed he shattered the aquarium, and the fish swam all over the new paperbacks Sir had bought for the library. The broken window could have happened to anyone, said Sir, but then Rocket had to be carted away to the Out-patients because he'd swallowed a drawing pin and it was stuck in his throat.

'Just tell,' groaned Sir, head in hands, 'me or anyone else who's curious, how anyone comes to swallow a drawing pin? Can you give me one good reason why he had a drawing pin in his mouth in the first place?'

When he came back Rocket was in his old place. Beside Trish.

'I spec you're pleased,' he beamed, 'now Rocket's back.'

The man standing at Sir's desk waited silently until we all stopped yacking and sat down. Then in walked Chief Sir, the Head Teacher, so we all stood up again.

'Good morning, children.'

'Good morning, Sir.' But we stared with question-mark faces at the new man.

'Now, this is Mr Carter, who will be teaching you this term. Sit down,' he continued through all the oohs and ahs. 'I trust that you have all had a refreshing holiday and are returned keen as mustard to throw yourselves into your studies. And, of course, to enjoy your last term here before leaving the nest and setting out for new schools, eh, young Moffat? Ah, I see young Moffat has not yet arrived. You recall I mentioned him to you, Mr Carter? A treat, a veritable treat in store for you. Not everyone has the good fortune in life to encounter such as young Moffat, or Rodney, I should say.'

I tried to catch Trish's eye and on succeeding wished I hadn't bothered for she looked like Nagaina, the cobra in *Rikki-Tikki-Tavi* when the mongoose seizes her eggs (one of my favourite stories).

Mr Carter said, 'Good morning, children,' and we all chorused back at him, except for Trish who cried out,

'Where's Mr Merchant? What's happened to him?'

'Mr Merchant had an accident . . .'

This time the gasp was enormous, with Trish crying oh, no, and looking as if she'd found out she was part of a Hammer horror film and not just watching one. 'He's not . . . dead, is he?'

'No, no, no, of course he isn't dead. Don't be so dramatic, Patricia. It isn't at all like that.'

There was a long pause while we waited for him to tell us about it, but he hummed a little tune, 'Lord of the Dance', it was. At last Trish could bear no more.

'What is it like, then?'

'He fell off the ladder when he was painting the landing ceiling, and has broken various bones, that's all.'

'All? It's terrible,' cried Trish.

'He's extremely disappointed not to be back at school with you all, and he'll do his utmost to return as soon as it's possible. In the meantime we have Mr Carter, who has so kindly stepped into the breach at very short notice . . .'

'What about the baby?' interrupted Trish, obviously not caring less about Mr Carter kindly stepping in at very short notice . . .

'What baby?'

'Mr Merchant was going to have a baby soon.'

'Was he really? How extraordinary. Are you sure, Patricia? Oh, ah, yes, I remember now. His wife, you mean, child. No, the baby hasn't arrived yet. All most unfortunate, but I'm sure that you will be more than adequately looked after by Mr Carter here, who has so splendidly come forward in our hour of need. And now I'll leave you to the delights of the morning. Every day a fresh source of wonder, I always say.'

He beamed at us all, then departed humming 'Slaughter on Tenth Avenue,' which isn't easy. In the classroom buzzing rose like bees swarming, Trish the Queen Bee about to take flight, go, leave. The new teacher rapped the table smartly.

'Settle down. I want to get to know you all.'

'I want to write to Mr Merchant,' Trish said, just like that, pushing it. 'Please,' she added, but too late.

'We have work to do first. Quiet now.'

16

And silence fell as he began to mark the register, and in that silence a noise could be heard, quietly at first, then louder and louder, clattering feet and a roaring sound, coming nearer, getting much louder, until the door crashed open and in shot Rocket as if catapulted, with Buggsy the caretaker right behind him.

'Found this young varmint on the bike shed roof,' he panted, slewing to a halt, as Rocket tripped over the nearest chair, rebounded off the next, hit one table, bounced off another, and finally came to rest on the centre display table still covered with specimens from last term's fossil-hunting expedition. Rocks, reference books, fossils and Rocket all

rearranged themselves in a shattering and spectacular spread over the table and the floor. Everyone in the class – well, nearly everyone – shrieked, Buggsy threw up his hands and went, Mr Carter stayed calm.

'Would you care to tell me your name?' he asked.

The ones who didn't immediately inform him were Rocket, Trish, me and Tam Lann. Judging from the stories he writes Tam has encountered many disasters, and as for Trish and me, we just know Rocket. Besides, the new Sir would find out only too soon. A while later, things were sorted out and a shaking Rocket settled by Trish.

'Trying to fly off the roof,' she whispered.

'Mm, I guessed,' I whispered back, for this new man looked as if he wouldn't miss a murmur. He marked the register, then walked round the class handing a small piece of card to each of us.

'So that I can get to know you more quickly I should like you to write your names on the cards I've given you, then sellotape them to your place on the table. Boys, you put your surnames, girls your Christian names.'

Trish shot like a jack-in-the-box out of her seat.

'But, Sir, we don't go in for that sort of thing here. Mr Merchant . . .'

He motioned her to sit down, then ignoring her completely, said,

'Neat writing, please, or I shan't be able to read your names.'

Trish banged down on to her chair, face flaming as red as her poppy-coloured hair.

'Do you think Sir will die?' asked Sandra Hayes, who's so dim she makes Rocket look like a genius, though maybe he is, he's certainly batty enough.

'Of course he won't die, stupid. You don't die from a broken arm.'

We stood under the old tree in the playground, talking, jabbering, all except Trish who was wearing silence like an old grey blanket, once she'd warned Rocket to stay put next to her and not do anything at all, including breathing.

'If he dies, do we have the day off for the funeral?' Sandra never knows when to stop.

'I'd like that,' nodded her mate, Susie. Trish made a low growling noise in her throat.

'Wonder if the baby will have Bonfire's red hair?'

'That'd be better than looking like Mr Merchant!'

'The new one's good-looking.'

'Dishy.' They giggled and Trish exploded.

'You blithering dead stupid lot of half witted morons! That man is AWFUL. You wait and see. In a week he'll have you saying, Yes Sir, No Sir, black's white Sir, grovel, grovel, creep, creep, scared stiff, frightened to breathe. And when he does, don't come to me moaning we thought he was dishy and what are you going to do about it, Trish?'

With that she stormed off. I looked at Tam Lann.

'She's in a mood 'cos Sir's not here. You know how she is.'

'Trish, she's often in a mood. Though I think that this time she may be right. Just wait and see.'

I leaned against the old tree. Sir told us it was a cypress, only now it had the wrong shape, for so many of its lower branches had been blown off by the gales or lopped off because they might be dangerous. One day it would fall down, or be cut down, and then our school would look just like all the other town schools. I stared up at the top branches, seeming to move into another, a different world of shape and light and space and darkness where everything was in another time, another pattern, not at all like the one I live and know with home and my mother, and school and the Moffats next door. A melody danced and jumped through my head, a jokey tune, dancing its feet off the ground with head up there among the birds and the branches. The tune laughed its way along, then Rocket pulled at my arm, a sad white-headed scarecrow, blown by a cold wind. Things weren't right and Rocket was sad. I grinned at him.

'Come on. I've found a smashin' picture of a pterodactyl,' and his face brightened from sad to mad, for Rocket loves pterodactyls, those earliest of flyers, and we went back to the classroom.

It was almost the end of the morning when Trish had another go.

'Please Mr Carter, we always used to stop a bit before the end of the morning and clear up and we had a poem or a story or sometimes a puzzle . . .'

'Patricia . . . Moffat, isn't it? I'd like to ask you something. Who is in charge of this class? You or I?'

Once more Trish's face flamed into sunset colours.

'You are,' she muttered at last.

'Then I suggest you leave the timetable to me. Just carry on with your Fletcher Maths, children, till the buzzer goes.'

We carried on.

4

What is the difference between teacher and Polo mints?
People like Polos.

Finally at three o'clock we finished copying notes off the board and put down our pens, Rocket by now a whiter shade of pale because he can't copy very much, his fingers get cramp – and his brain. Trish and I did bits for him when Sir wasn't looking in our direction, but it's not easy.

Mr Carter looked at his watch. 'I think we could possibly spare time for letters to Mr Merchant now.'

Paper was given out, but by this time we'd written so much during the day – mainly copying – that we'd gone beyond and the last thing we wanted to do was to write a letter to anyone. Still, we started off once again, and I tried to get a lot into mine so that he'd feel cheered up and want to come back as soon as poss, and then Rocket needn't be white white and Trish red red all the time. I wrote out a joke, never easy for me, drew a picture of Rocket as Tarzan, added a few mythical beasts and monsters of my own, and scribbled some musical notes that made a message I hoped he'd understand, though he always says he's about as musical as a falling ton of bricks. Oh, and get better, come back soon.

'It won't do. That kind of thing won't do at all,' said Mr Carter.

He was, of course, looking at Rocket's, and I suppose it's

hard for anyone who doesn't know him to realize that what he'd drawn was a crowd of smiling animals round Sir in bed with his arm in a sling. Underneath he'd written, 'I hop yuo is betr soon, lov form ROCKET.'

Mr Carter cast his eyes over one or two more, then said, 'Take them all back. They won't do. I'll write a suitable one on the board, then you can copy it to get the correct format, adding a few personal points of interest at the end. I'm sure you'll be able to think of some, Patricia,' and he smiled thinly at Trish, who seemed about to explode all of the time instead of just some of it.

At last, knackered, we gathered up the letters and put them on the desk to be posted. They all began, 'I am sorry to hear that you have met with an accident . . .'

'A funny thing to meet with,' Tam whispered. 'D'you

think it was coming along the road when he met it?'

'No, up the stairs and along the landing, just out for a stroll.'

'Quiet, now. Tidy your tables and put your chairs up ready to go home.'

'I hope Sir doesn't get a heart attack from all the excitement when he reads those,' Trish muttered bitterly.

The day that had lasted for half a century ended at last. Trish rushed out of school and I didn't try to catch up in case she was crying. I walked home with Rocket though walk was hardly the word for it, since he ran on top of three walls, climbed a lamppost, tried to fly off a bank, cat-sprang about twenty yards, then sat on a hydrant sign refusing to budge, muttering how much he hated Carter. I thought I'd better stay with him and at last we arrived at the Moffats, though I didn't go in. Better see Trish later, I thought, get practice out of the way, maybe write down the tree/Rocket/scarecrow tune. By then she'll've calmed down and wouldn't take it out on me, I hoped.

But it was all different. My mother was home, earlier than expected. And Dorothy her manager/secretary. And presents for me, super prezzies like my mother always brings . . . a computer . . . and a box of chocolates for the Moffats . . .

Once there was a teacher at school who used to go on and on boringly about my mother, talking and asking me questions, which I never knew how to answer, so I just stood there, hating it and hoping she'd belt up. I hated her as well, for she was horrible to Trish and Rocket while she made this fuss of me, so some of the kids took the mickey, calling me Creep and Charlie Darling, till Rocket went for them and was sent to Chief Sir, since one of them had told his parents that Rocket turned into a big white werewolf who ate people,

23

and there was trouble. But all the time I thought the real cause of the trouble was this talk about my mother when there was no cause to mention her, and Mrs Somers, that was the teacher's name, she's left now, saying to me, 'What is a famous mother really like when she's at home?' laughing and glittering her teeth.

'Tired,' I said and wouldn't say any more, and she got very angry with me though she tried not to show it. And it's true. My mother is always tired when she gets home because of the travelling and meeting people as well as playing in front of audiences. She usually only wants to sleep, not talk much, so we don't. She smiles at me and says she's glad to be back. And I'm pleased as well, the lonely feeling goes away.

'She isn't grand, is she?' Trish said once. 'When she's not done up like that time we saw her on telly, she looks just like those mums who are always cooking and putting out wellies for their kids to have adventures in and waiting for them to come home from camping . . .'

'She isn't like that, though. She gets jolly up-tight if you don't do what she wants.'

'Mine's not like that either. I wonder if there are any left nowadays? She went bananas last night cos Chas has got another bike. You should've heard her though I'm glad you didn't.'

'I did.' Trish's mum has a voice like a saw hitting a rusty nail.

'Through the wall, I suppose. It was all hell let loose, I can tell you. She started on our Dad because he'd forgotten to post the pools coupon. Only hope for us lot, she said, and since it was the only work he ever did, he might've remembered it.'

My mother listened to me play, said fine, and that I could

have a set of drums next birthday, which I wanted anyway, and also I'd got this idea that though Rocket's tone-deaf, he might be able to feel the rhythm somehow . . . just an idea. The instrument I most want I don't tell her about, as I'm scared of what she'll say, what she'll think. Besides, Dorothy always seems to be there with us and I don't want to say anything that matters in front of her. She thinks I should be as inconspicuous as poss – and I do my best but that's not good enough for her – the sooner I'm out of the way at boarding school the better. Get him off your hands, I've heard her say. I wanted Charlie to go to my old school, my mother says, I was so happy there. Rose-coloured spectacles sniffs Dorothy. No, I don't want Charlie to go away too early, my mother continues, and Dorothy sniffs again. Artists can't afford sentimentality, she says. Your trouble is, Marian, you've got a little bit of a soft centre and it won't do. Oh, I always liked those best, especially the cherry ones, my mother laughs, and I can tell Dorothy is annoyed again cos she bangs things.

Most of all Dorothy wants us to move to a grand house, more suitable, not in a run-down area with a crowd of no-good layabouts next door, and those hooligans, meaning my fiendish friends, Trish and Rocket. It's Dorothy who buys the expensive bath oil that Trish likes.

'Funny how it goes down. It can't be Charlie using it. He hardly even washes his face . . . I wonder if it's Hortense. I never quite trust her. I shall have a word . . .'

But I shan't. As Trish says, I'm secretive, never letting on about anything I don't have to.

5

At the next concert the school orchestra will play
*   Beethoven.*
I bet Beethoven loses.

Next day there was another change. Old Champers had
always taken us for music, while Sir took his class for Games,
but Mr Carter announced that he would conduct his own
music lessons. He was keen on music, he told us. Music was
His Subject, he said, sounding as if he owned it personally.
Now old Champers may not be the world's best pianist, but
his lessons were great, with good songs and fun with different
instruments, percussion, wind, brass, home-made maraccas,
pieces of string tied to bits of wood. Champers could get a
tune from anything. And he never took any notice of me or
mentioned my mother, so I could enjoy myself. Even Rocket
liked music lessons and learnt to play *Frère Jacques* on the
recorder, a miracle if ever there was one.

That day had off notes from the start. Rocket wasn't
going to school, he said, sitting folded knees to chin behind
the big chair in the Moffat kitchen, barricaded in behind
Toyah's plastic bath, the broken washing machine, and an
old pram. He wanted to go and buy some polythene sheets
to make some wings.

'I'll get you a dustbin liner from school. That'll do just as
well,' promised Trish. Rocket picked up a plastic flowerpot
as if to throw at her.

'I'm not coming to school with you.'

'Look, Charlie's waiting for you and it's getting late. We've got to go. You can't mitch because you don't like the new teacher.'

'I can. You see.'

Trish went out, then came back carrying Toyah in baggy pyjamas. She launched herself over the chair, pulled Rocket's hair and bit his ear.

'Ow,' he yelled, catapulting out of the corner, Toyah still clamped to the ear.

'Grab his arm, Charlie,' Trish bellowed and together we got him to the door. 'Let go,' she ordered Toyah, who then

grabbed her Weeties packet off the table and spilt them all over the floor. Somehow we got away, and Rocket, resigned but with snapping teeth and hair on end, came along with us to school where we plonked him down between us, hoping Sir Carter, as Trish had christened him, wouldn't notice, though it seemed unlikely as Rocket looked as inconspicuous as a white lamb in a flock of black sheep. Fortunately it was his morning to go to Mrs Lane, along with Sandra, for extra reading and language work, so he'd be out of the firing area. After the register he and Sandra stood up to go. Sir looked up from what he was studying. He spent a lot of time looking at things while we waited.

'What are you two doing?'

'Mrs Lane's. Extra reading,' smiled Sandra. Mrs Lane is round and cuddly like a duvet and gives them sweets when they try extra hard. Brian Cooper was wild when he was told he'd come on enough to rejoin the main stream.

'Falling rolls have necessitated a reduction in staff numbers and Mrs Lane will not be with us this term. So sit down, both of you. And, Moffat – do you have to come to school looking quite so disgusting? Go to the cloakroom, wash your face and tidy your hair. I've no doubt school uniform is too much to ask but at least tuck your shirt in and tie your shoe-laces. Patricia Moffat, why is your hand up? What is it now? Can't it wait?'

'I don't think so, Sir. What did you mean by what you just said? Before the tidy up bit?'

'I made myself perfectly clear. Sandra and Moffat stay here this morning.'

'I meant the other bit. About falling rolls or something. What you really mean are the education cuts, don't you, Sir?'

Trish always manages to sound stroppy even if she's just

interested so I wasn't surprised when Sir said, 'It's not your place to discuss such matters . . .'

'Mr Merchant did . . .'

Sir's blue eyes blazed and his mouth thinned. Tam and I went to kick Trish at the same time, only we kicked each other instead. Not a good day.

'Julia Wenham, give out these books to the Group A children . . .' Here, he read out a list of our table minus Rocket. '. . . and this set to Group B . . .' and he started on another list. 'And what is it now, Patricia?'

'We didn't have A, B, C groups before . . .' Trish flamed. 'We were different . . .'

'Your trouble is you think you're different. When your teacher comes back you can be what he wants, but with me you are Groups A, B, C, D, with Sandra and Moffat on their own. Is that clear? Then, get out your exercise books and begin. At the beginning, Patricia, and work straight on. Lewis, go and see what's happened to Moffat.'

I looked round to see who this Lewis was, then realized with surprise that it was me. So I moved at speed to the cloakroom, praying Rocket hadn't decided this was the time to try flying home.

But he was there all right, looking out of the window and warbling, Pooooooooooooor Rooooooocket in an off-key grating noise that set your teeth on edge.

'Sir says you've got to come on.' He looked at me as if I was a worm which is how I felt.

'No. I'm gonna stay 'ere for ever-aneveraneveranever. So there.'

Desperate, I searched round in my pocket and came up with a fluffy mint. 'Yours,' I coaxed, 'if you come.' It was a complete waste of time.

'You're joking. You've had that for years.'

'OK OK OK. I know. But if you don't come we're both in trouble.'

He smiled at me, very kindly and as if he was a hundred years old. 'For you, Charlie, anything,' and walked quite calmly out of the cloakroom and back to the classroom. Feeling weak, I followed and sat down where our Group A was silently working its way through oh, no, not again, *New and Improved English for Primary Schools*.

'D'you remember when we did it over and over in Mrs Somers's class?' muttered Trish, shooting down the page at the speed of light.

'Quiet there. This is a language lesson so there should be no talking AT ALL.'

After a minute, 'You should see what the rest have got. *Reading for Finding Out* and *Fun with Word Families*,' hissed Trish. I just wished she'd belt up and let us get on with it in quiet miserable boredom. Too late.

'*A* table will stay on to work at break as they are apparently incapable of maintaining an orderly silence.'

He turned to Rocket, still standing by his desk.

'Bring that table over here so that it's near to me. Then you and Sandra can copy this passage in your best handwriting.'

Rocket moved like someone who volunteered to cross the Atlantic in a bath tub on his own, but has suddenly got doubts. At last they were settled. I watched them, as even Sandra was more interesting than *New and Improved* . . .

'I can't read this,' said Rocket.

'Nor me,' Sandra chimed in.

For a moment a look of mad desperation flashed over Sir's face, and I almost felt sorry for him, cos I know what life with Rocket can do to people.

But he sat up even straighter and said,

'I didn't ask you to read it. Just copy it for now.'

I finished five or six exercises, then noticed Trish had dared to stop writing and get out a library book. So I did the same. After a while Mr Carter came round the class to check our work, said mine was satisfactory and asked me to read to him. In a minute he snatched the book off me.

'Whatever is this book? Where did you get this?'

'It's a follow-up to one we read in class with Mr Merchant, funny and about school, a school like ours.'

'I don't care for the tone of it at all. I don't like its language. Leave it. I'll get you a reader.'

Reader? But I'm the reader. Not the book. He came back with *Coral Island* so I told him I already knew it.

'That doesn't matter. Read it to me . . . Ah, that's better. In fact, you don't read at all badly, Lewis. You have a go.'

This was to Trish, who was also reading the book that Sir Carter had objected to. This time his eyebrows rose even higher as he took it off her and fetched *Little Women* from the bookcase. But poor Rocket. He was sent down to the first school for an old Infant Reader they don't use any more.

Oh, a long, long morning. Rocket, white and wild, burst out at play time and knocked down a visiting School Governor, which caused a lot of upset in many ways. Not that we, Group A in all our splendour, knew anything of this, for we were back with *New and Improved*, wading through a chapter on Creative Writing.

'Destructive writing's what I need,' growled Trish. 'Every letter a bullet.'

'I think you don't know what you say, Trish,' Tam murmured, but Sir returned with his coffee and we 'ad to 'ave 'ush. I was looking forward to the dinner hour – at least I could eat instead of using a pen – but afterwards we found

Rocket trembling with two hundred lines to write, and his hands too achey to manage he told us. Groaning, Trish and I mucked in, until some creep from the third year told Mr Carter and we received a hundred each of our own. Tam Lann came in like a shadow, collected paper and biro and departed to do some for us under the tree in the playground where nobody noticed. I told you he was clever.

'At least it's music with old Champers this afternoon,' I said to Trish, hoping to cheer her up for she was ferociously silent, mouth turned down like a trap. Music might make a miracle, Sir, Mr Merchant back at school, all at peace, but even without miracle-making, music would make it seem better, music always does.

But as I told you it wasn't old Champers for music, it was Sir Carter. His face and look were printed on my brain by now. Just the day before yesterday I didn't know he existed. You walk along a road you know, turn the corner and this dragon rears up roaring out of a cave you never realized was there and nothing's the same again, ever. He looked excited, shining with energy. Once more he told us Music was His Subject. Well? It might be all right. Maybe. Who knows? Perhaps he'd be as good with His Music as Mr Merchant with stories and poetry and history . . . Give it a spin. But keep quiet, keep very quiet, Charlie boy.

'I hope that you will enjoy this enormously, that it will be a whole new meaningful experience for you, opening up fresh worlds. Now, this afternoon we'll start off with singing something you know well, "Green Grow the Rushes, Oh".'

The class, now full of enthusiasm, for we wanted to do well, wanted to like a new teacher, wanted him to like us, to say we were good, opened up at full throttle. Champers used to say we were a nice crowd, he liked us. Rocket also wanted to make a new start, I think, to show he was trying, for he lifted up his great white head and sang at maximum volume, like some mad dog baying at the full moon. It was terrible, worse than anything you could imagine. I leaned away from the awful din as far as I could, but it didn't help much.

The new teacher had a baton in his hand. He swept it down, his face full of storms, and we stopped in a straggly fashion, Rocket warbling on till he realized everyone else was quiet, then gazing round bewildered, worried. And so was I. For I was scared at what I saw in our new teacher's face, afraid, for he was shaking like Rocket shakes, and his face had gone white like Rocket's, but he was our teacher. Not Rocket. He pushed the end of the baton into Rocket's bony chest as he cringed back.

'Are you doing it deliberately?' he cried. 'Are you ruining my music on purpose?'

'No, Sir, he doesn't know how bad he is,' cried Trish.

'Be quiet and don't interfere. Let him speak. Are you deliberately making that noise?' and he screwed the baton even further into Rocket.

But speaking was beyond Rocket. His mouth tried to form the words but the muscles couldn't. Trish turned to me, eyes swivelling like the eyes of the dogs in that story about a soldier and a tinder box. I couldn't bear it. I spoke.

'He's ... he's got no ear for music at all. I think he's totally tone-deaf. Anything musical is inaudible to him, so he can't keep on a note because he doesn't really know what one is, so he makes noises he hopes are like everybody else's. And gets them all wrong.'

'What can you possibly know about it?' he snapped, but he took the baton away, and he stopped shaking.

'Go. Wait outside,' he told Rocket, who scrambled for the door. 'The rest of you – I want something better.'

And it was. Out of terror.

6

Knock, knock.
Who's there?
Noise.
Noise who?
Noise to see you after all this time.

'You know there isn't one girl in that story he's reading to us,' said Trish, as we sat in deep gloom and despondency on some old boxes behind the Great Nettle Barrier. Even Tarzan's tree top wails weren't as loud as usual.

'I read it years ago and didn't think much of it then. It's really boring. I bet his teacher read it to him when he was at school.'

'Fancy him at school. Yuck. Charlie, we've got to do something.'

'But what? You can't do anything about teachers. They're an Act of God. You're either lucky or unlucky, and our luck ran out. No, Trish, there ain't nuttin we can do. Teachers are like that hymn, Chief Sir's favourite, you know, "Immortal, all-powerful . . ." '

'Invisible, you mean,' giggled Trish. 'I wish he was.'

'I wish I was. Hey, that's given me an idea . . .'

'Great. Tell us. It's not often you get ideas except about music. We could use some ideas.'

'No, forget it. It wouldn't work and it might be dangerous . . .'

'Oh, Charlie, you are a pain. And you've got your sly look again.'

'I'm not sly!'

'Yes you are. Sometimes.'

'I AM NOT SLY!'

'OK OK. Cool it. I'm sorry. I didn't mean . . .'

'Yes, you did, you did.'

'Oh, belt up. Listen. I *have* got an idea. Want to hear it? Well, do you or don't you?'

'Please yourself . . .'

'Oh, be like that, then. I don't care . . .'

'We had your teacher for singing and our class liked him,' announced Bernadette, joining us with Toyah in tow. Toyah sat in the grass and played with a worm, poor worm, fancy being that unlucky.

'Your class are creeps. You'll find out soon enough what he's really like.'

'He said I sang remarkably well,' Bernadette went on.

'Yuck. I'm off. To see Sir. That was my idea, Charlie. He'll tell us what to do. Are you coming?'

'I am,' yodelled Rocket, crashing down from the tree. 'Wait for me.'

'Do you have to? Charlie, make up your mind what you're doing.'

'I don't know if I can. There's my practice and my mother's having people in for a meal and there's one I've got to meet, she says . . .'

'Huh, you see. I tell you Charlie's a snob,' sniffed Bernadette.

'Leave it, Bernie. He can't help his rotten home life.'

'What's rotten about it? Charlie Lewis has got it made. I can sing as well as he can play, but they won't send me to a grand posh music school, will they?'

36

'But they might. I could ask my mother to hear you sing, Bernadette.'

'Don't bother. I can make Number One on my own. Who needs you? I just want you to know that you're spoilt, Charlie Lewis. Come on, Toyah.'

Toyah hurled a worm at me so I moved with some speed. My mother said I could go if I got back by eight, so I caught up Trish and Rocket at the bus stop. My mother had also given me flowers for Bonfire and chocolates for Sir, just as well as we'd forgotten about taking something.

The bus driver stared at Rocket, arms folded over the steering wheel.

'I know you. And I'm not sure I'm letting you on. Five people complained last time.'

'But I only flew down the stairs,' protested Rocket, hurt.

'I'll look after him,' protested Trish, batting her eyelashes up and down, which she thinks makes her look like the Cricklepit answer to Miss World, but which really makes her look as if she's got a fly in her eye. The driver let us on and we climbed upstairs, Rocket muttering to himself all the way.

When we arrived at the house, Bonfire, Mrs Merchant I mean – we used to call her that because she's got red hair, though paler than Trish's – let us in, a funny shape but smiling at us.

'Come right in. It's lovely to see you. He needs someone to talk to – he's like a bear with a sore head. He says he's never climbing another ladder if he lives to be ninety. Go in there.'

Sir sat bandaged like an Egyptian mummy.

'Oh, no, not him,' he cried at the sight of Rocket. 'Stay there, lad, on the other side of the room and don't move, for I feel very delicate at the moment. Janet, can you fetch some old Beanos for him to look at? Good lad. Just stay still and we shall be fine. I hope.'

Trish had already plonked herself down on the floor beside him and was busy writing 'Trish loves Sir' on one of his plasters. On the other one she wrote 'Trish hates Sir Carter.'

'Are you saying you don't care for your new teacher?'

'You're quick,' Trish grinned.

'Poor man. He has all the sympathy I can spare from myself at the moment.'

Words poured from Trish; unfair, cruel, boring, stupid, tyrant, chauvinist male pig were just some of them.

'What a remarkable fellow. I wish I'd managed to be all those things to the class. Makes me quite envious. Here, let's have some of Charlie's mother's best Swiss chocolates, splendid – she must be home, Charlie – while I contemplate this fiend in the dreaded likeness of a teacher.'

We sat and stuffed ourselves, and drank orange juice. Peace fell. At last Mr Merchant said, 'I don't know what you are expecting from me, Trish. A miracle, perhaps? But there's nothing I can do sitting here like an Assembly kit that hasn't stuck properly. He's your teacher and I can't interfere.'

Chug, chug, chug, chug glurked the computer in Trish's brain.

'No, you're dead right,' she said at last. 'You can't do a thing. But you can tell me what to do.'

'Absolutely nothing. You just have to put up with him and get on with it. You could even try that fair play you always talk about so much.'

'Is that all?'

'Afraid so. Cheer up. It won't last for ever. Any minute now I shall be back among you and you'll be sighing for the happy days with Mr Carter. I think I shall be particularly

38

devilish and tyrannical upon return. In fact, I can use this leisure time to invent some truly fiendish schemes. I wonder if I could ring up Mr Carter and ask for a few tips . . .'

'William,' said Bonfire, warningly.

Trish sighed but she was grinning again.

'I shall have to go soon. I'm sorry,' I said.

We made our way to the door.

'Oh, good luck with the cricket team, Trish,' Sir called after us.

'You're fat,' Rocket said to Bonfire in the doorway. 'Not like you used to be. You'll have to slim.'

'Oh, Rocket, you are funny,' she laughed. And he was pleased.

Home was grand, glittering and gleaming, lights, flowers, bottles, people. Dorothy had been busy. I could hear her voice as soon as I came in. I wanted Trish to come in with me, but Hortense kept her out. I tried to slip upstairs but Hortense fetched me. This is Charlie, said my mother, and this, Charlie, is Walter Schliemann. You remember, Charlie, we talked about him, you do remember don't you? Yes, I remembered my mother talking but I hadn't listened. He was little and old, a mole in velvet, a white beard at the end of a long chin. He took me away from all the others.

'Play,' he said.

'What?'

'Anything. Everything.'

So I did. For a long time. At the end he said thank you and went away. I didn't want to follow him back to all those people, so I went to bed and put on records from the secret collection, wearing my headphones in case anyone came in. My mother came up very late to say good night, smelling of wine and Dorothy's bath oil.

7

What should you do when you see Dracula,
Frankenstein's monster, four werewolves, two
vampires and the Incredible Hulk all in one room?
Keep your fingers crossed and hope that it's a fancy
dress party.

So we lay low, stayed quiet, kept a low profile as we covered page after page with writing, worked out dozens of sums in our exercise books, read *Coral Island* and *Little Women* and listened to Mr Carter reading us a story which as Trish said had no girls in it at all. We did no Art and Craft, no poetry, no drama, no History, no model-making, didn't use the computers or the tape recorders or the musical instruments, went on no expeditions. Science was Mr Carter showing us an experiment, then copying his notes from the board, we did no practical work in Maths, and PE was exercises and vaults.

From time to time someone objected, got stroppy, but Trish kept silent and without her back-up resistance soon crumbled. Mind you, he had a fan club by now, creeps and super-creeps, the yes Sir, no Sir, can I help you, Sir, hang around the desk, Sir, shall I watch what Rocket's doing and tell you, Sir, brigade.

'I have fingers of steel,' said Tam, 'from all this copying off the board.'

'What a remarkably quiet class,' cried Chief Sir, sweeping

in, eyes everywhere, bushy eyebrows twitching. 'I wouldn't have recognized M4.'

Mr Carter smiled. 'A quiet atmosphere is conducive to learning, I always find.'

'Quite. I perceive that you have my young friend Rodney Moffat tucked well away in a corner.'

'It seemed best. Both for him and for the rest of the class.'

Chief Sir headed for Rocket and peered at his work. 'I see you're getting down a splendid number of words on that page, Rocket, isn't it? Now, shall we see if you can read back to me all those words you've copied down?'

All the class were watching, Trish wearing her rat-trap mouth.

'He won't be able to. I hope Chief Sir isn't angry,' she muttered.

And she was right. He couldn't.

'I don't think he's been sufficiently stretched in the past,' we heard Sir Carter say. Rocket looked terrified.

'The rack, the rack,' murmured Tam.

'He's long and skinny enough already,' I muttered back, and we all got the giggles. Sir Carter glared at us.

'I thought he sometimes worked with his sister – that she helped him along a bit – a capable child, that one,' Chief Sir said, then began one of his humming sessions, which I tried to catch. It sounded like Number One on last week's chart, but surely it couldn't be unless I was going crazy. Or Chief Sir? What was he up to? Last time he'd prowled around like this we'd been in Mrs Somers's class and we ended up on a Junior Outward Bound course.

'We could try that,' said Mr Carter. 'Patricia, come over here by your brother. Read that page to him and then go over it with him. Come along, now.'

Trish, who had leapt up like a flaming torch, drooped and died into old grey ashes as she realized Rocket wasn't being welcomed back but she was being banished to the dark corner away from us all.

'But . . .' she began, then stopped, and picking up her books, but dropping pens, ruler and felt-tips, clatter, crash, she clomped her way over to Rocket, slower than a tortoise on crutches. Chief Sir beamed at her, then told us all that *Pilgrim's Progress* was a best seller in his long ago and far away days, and made his exit, humming what was quite definitely last week's Number One, the song banned in America. But then I never did get the hang of Chief Sir. If you mention him to my mother she just smiles all over her face and says oh, what a lovely man, which goes to support my theory that all grown-ups are insane, got to be. How anyone could think Chief Sir lovely beats me, mad, yes, crazy, yes, lovely, question mark. Cheered, I scrawled on my jotter cover, 'Chief Sir is strong, Chief Sir is gentle, Chief Sir is Kind, And also mental,' and passed it over to Tam who smiled his oriental smile.

'Bring that up to me, Lewis.'

'What, Sir? My work, Sir?'

'No, what you wrote just then.'

So I took it up to him, there not being much else I could do, not that he could really object to a corny old verse like that. In fact, it was Mr Merchant who told it to us in the first place. Mr Carter stared at the words for a long time, watched by the full audience of a class bored out of its tiny communal mind by over an hour of English Comprehension. They really wanted something to happen. Me roasted over a slow fire, probably. Anything to make a change.

'I suppose you think that's funny,' he said at last.

'Not very.'

43

'Well, you can exercise your undeveloped sense of humour by writing out in the lunch hour, "I must learn to distinguish between wit and stupidity." Do you understand that, Lewis?'

A sigh went up from the class. Disappointment, I supposed, and I felt wicked. 'No, Sir. It's too hard for me, Sir. Would you explain it, please?'

He started off, 'Oh, heavens, you lot . . . virtually illiterate. It means . . .' then he stopped and looked sharply at me.

'Go and sit down. And don't cause any more trouble.'

Trish was to be allowed back to our table for music, which cheered her up, but did nothing for Rocket, who sat there, dead miserable, hating being left on his own all the time, not allowed to join in any of the music. Sir was going to hear all the rest of us sing, weed out the sheep from the goats, he said. So one by one we stood and sang, while Rocket mouthed 'poor Rocket' over and over as he sat and stared at the spellings he was supposed to be learning. There was one laugh. When it was Trish's turn I knew she'd said she wasn't going to try, but Trish loves singing, though she's nowhere near as good as Bernadette, and she got caught and sang her hardest, so that old Carter said at the end,

'Good, that was good. You've got a really pretty little girl's voice,' and she sat down, her face as sour as a lemon.

When it came to my turn I'd already decided to be a goat, so I sang flat, not too much, just nicely off. I was worried he might guess, for I knew my mother would've, but he just said sit down Lewis, we'll have to manage with what we've got, which is about five of you – he named them, leaving me out – with any feeling or ability for music.

'They will have to carry the rest along.'

44

The rest put on the bored look that he was surely beginning to get to know, by now.

'Now we're going to learn a very old and famous song. It's called 'Nymphs and Shepherds'. Write the words down as I read them out to you. Who was that groaning?'

'Most of the class,' muttered Trish. Then after a moment or two —

'I can't believe it.'

We wrote slowly on, hindered by those who kept asking Sir what he'd said, please would he repeat that?

'He's not making us learn *this*, is he?'

'He is.'

'It's the worst song ever written. Not even you know a worse one, do you, Charlie?'

'There's one called "Ruddier Than The Cherry". That's bad.'

'What's this about Flora's holiday? She should be so lucky. I wish it was my holiday.'

Five children were asking how you spelt Flora, I can't keep up cried someone else, what's a nymph and so on. In the end the words went up on the board. And Mr Carter started to sing it, then play each bit on the piano, while we had to follow him note by note, bar by bar, phrase by phrase, then line by line. It was absolutely diabolical, stinking awful. The class hated the words and didn't think much of the music. Notes leaked out like drips from a leaky sewer outlet. I found it hilarious, for I thought about all the times they'd been out at play when I'd been practising studies and scales, so I sang away, taking care to be just flat all the time, which I found interesting. Then I took a look at Mr Carter's face and the laughs left me, for he looked weird, bonkers, like the time he was so angry with Rocket. I turned away to look at Rocket and saw him

45

slip out of the room, oh no, trouble, trouble, I thought.

'Trish, Rocket's gone,' I sang among the music, or rather the awful row.

Sir rapped with his baton and shouted:

'That was appalling. Appalling. I have never heard anything so dreadful. Now, concentrate on what you are doing, for you are going to get this right if we have to stay here all day. I will not have you wrecking my music.'

But it's not your music I wanted to say, it's everybody's music, and if anyone's wrecking it it's you, making everybody miserable so they can't enjoy it.

Julia put up a hand, 'Sir, it was games time five minutes ago.'

'No one is going out to games until I've got this perfect, the way I want it. Patricia, open the windows. You're all going to sleep. Right, breathe in, breathe out . . .'

This time the singing was a little better, but suddenly the door crashed open and in walked Rocket, wearing his games kit, dirty, rucked up, shoes on the wrong feet, but changed and ready at the correct time. He was proud of his kit and enjoyed games because he could fly up and down the pitch. Despite the open window the air was thick about us, so I could hardly breathe; oh no, murmured Trish. I bent my head, wanting to keep out of trouble, hoping, willing that he wouldn't get angry with Rocket. The bright blue eyes in the big pale face alarmed me. He took two strides towards the untidy figure and the room fell silent as fear stretched out a frosty finger and touched us all. I thought I could hear my heart pounding, then he checked and took a deep breath. I know about deep breaths from playing wind instruments and this was a very big one. A long pause, then he said quietly:

'Take off your kit, Moffat. You won't be needing it.

There's no games lesson today. We're going to practise this song until it's perfect. If it kills me.'

'Or us,' whispered Tam.

The week ended. Trish came home with me and tried out the computer, eyes swivelling with excitement. I left her programming away, and tried to get further with the pattern in the tree, putting it into a melody and rhythm completely different from anything I've done before, like using another base in Maths.

'Yuck. That sounds revolting. You gone deaf or somethin'?' cried Trish, coming in.

'Push off,' I snarled.

47

'Play one I like – the tune you did about Sir. "The Joker".'

'OK, OK. But I do like trying out something new and strange, you know, else it gets boring.'

'Let it. It's the boring ones I like.'

So I played the song for Sir and then took the mickey out of 'Nymphs and Shepherds', and we fell about until Rocket's face splodged itself against the window-pane, searching for us, so we rushed out to get him away fast before Hortense found him. We let him be Tarzan then, swinging through the trees, with Bernadette as Jane, no way am I going to be that boring twit, Trish had said, so she became the villain trying to capture the chimp for vivisection. It was a toss-up between Toyah and me who was to be the chimp, but she got called away by her mother so it had to be me. What a rotten scenario this is, cried Trish, but Rocket thought it great. So was the weekend, the only trouble being that it came to an end.

8

What did the monster eat after his teeth had been
  pulled out?
The dentist.

Rocket came quietly to school on Monday, and Mr Carter
was amiable. Could he be getting used to us? Or we to him?
And on the way home Trish grinned like the Cheshire Cat,
as if she knew something I didn't, yuck.

'What's got into you?' I growled at last as she was
obviously dying to tell me.

She laughed. 'Wait till you hear.'

'Out with it, then.'

'I heard old Champers talking to Lord Carter. So I
listened.'

'You always do, you nosey parker. It's disgusting.'

'I have to know what's going on or I can't operate
properly, keep my eye on things.'

'You can't operate properly anyway.'

'You want to hear this or . . .?'

'Oh, just get on with it . . .'

'OK, then. Well, Sir Carter big'ead was moaning and
carrying on about us, didn't think much of us, no proper
spirit, no self-discipline, and so on and so on, the usual . . .'

'You didn't waste your time listening to that, did you?'

'Hang about, Charlie. Then he said we didn't have much
talent, that Sandra and I and Alex could sing a bit . . .'

'I knew he was tone-deaf . . .'

'But we weren't really up to much, which is rubbish, because I'm as good as our Bernie any day and everyone raves about her.'

'But you're not.'

'Not what?'

'As good as Bernadette. She's in a different league. I can't stand the sight of her but she stops me in my tracks when she sings.'

'Do you want to hear my news or not?'

'I can't stop you now so you might as well get on with it.'

'Right. Where was I?'

'Getting round to admitting at last that Bernadette can sing better than you.'

'Shut up. Boring, boring. But this is what I want to tell you. Old Champers said, "But you've got Charlie Lewis . . ." '

'Oh, ah, no.'

'So his lordship said, "What's with Lewis then? What's so special about him? I don't care for him much." '

'And you said that I didn't care much for him either.'

'Course I didn't. I was round the corner out of sight, sorting books for Miss Plum, stupid.'

'Get on with it. Tell me the worst.'

'Old Champers sounded cross and he said . . . oh, you'd never guess . . .'

'Oh, I bet I would worse luck.'

' "Lewis, ha, he's only got perfect pitch, plays more instruments than you've had hot dinners, wrote the music for last year's school pantomime, and his mother is . . . wait for it . . ." '

'Oh, no, not again . . .'

' "Marian Forrest, the pianist." '

I closed my eyes. If I couldn't see Trish opening and

closing her mouth, perhaps I couldn't hear her either.

'What's the matter? Charlie? Don't you think it was great? I peered round the corner and there was King Carter looking as if he'd been . . . nuked . . .'

'Trish, don't say that . . .'

'Why not? Old Champs looked really pleased. Don't think he likes him much, as if anyone could. Good ole Charlie. Our claim to fame, and him making us all out to be so stoopid.'

I didn't answer. She rabbited on. And on. 'Marian Forrest, he said over and over.'

'I can't think why. She isn't exactly the Beatles or Princess Diana, is she?'

'But music's His Subject. He keeps telling us. So he'd be bound to know about her. "Marian Forrest," he went on, "not here. She can't be." '

' "Well, no, she's not here a great deal," ' said Champers, 'because she's always travelling, but her home is here. The Head knows her well. She came back to her old home when her marriage broke up, oh, sorry, Charlie.'

'Feel free. After all, I don't have feelings.'

'Well, my mum says you're better off without fathers. Charlie, why are you pulling that face? Anyway, King Kong . . .'

'Who?' Trish was driving me nearly mad.

'Him. Carter. He asked what about your name being Lewis. I told you he was stoopid, and Champers explained you'd kept your dad's name, and then he said he didn't believe you'd got perfect pitch, you sang flat. Want to know what Champers said to that?'

'No.'

'He said that's just the sort of thing you would do if you thought you could get away with it. That you could be very awkward and secretive. So you see. I'm not the only one who thinks so, Charlie. Charlie?'

'Leave it, Trish. Leave it!' And I ran and ran to put Trish and Mr Carter and everything all behind me, ran to the music that didn't jab and poke at you, but welcomed you and wound round you, weaving its spell, and after I'd listened a while the mad monster theme that had banged and crashed and battered the inside of my head quietened down into peace.

Hortense was shrieking and gobbling like a farmhouse turkey as I made my way to the back door where Trish, Rocket, Bernadette, Duwayne and even Toyah stood in a heap being told to go away and taking no notice.

'Tell zem zey cannot stay. Eet eez eemposseeble, all ov zem 'ere. Eeet weell not do. Zey weell break zingz. Go away . . . naughtee cheeldren.'

I could hear Trish saying, 'Sorry, Charlie. Sorry, sorry, didn't mean to hurt your feelings – being so many of us, we don't have them the same . . .'

'Go away, naughtee cheeldren,' cried Hortense. I couldn't look at Trish, I was too ashamed. Their mother always said come in, Charlie . . .

'Belt up, you stupid cow,' I shouted. 'These are my friends.'

I didn't know my mother was standing right behind me till she spoke.

'Charlie's friends are always welcome here. Hortense, I think I can hear the phone ringing. Perhaps you could answer it, please. Come in, all of you.'

'Thank you, Mrs Lewis,' Trish replied, 'but we thought Charlie might like to come for a feast in our garden as we've made some cakes for him.'

With everyone beaming at me as if they'd gone barmy I could only say yes, though I knew the cakes would taste as if they were straight from the cement mixer. My mother smiled and patted Toyah. I just hoped she wouldn't get bitten.

'You must all come and have tea with me.'

Something niggled, something I should remember, oh yes . . . that was it, Bernadette's snide remarks. I started to speak but Trish is always quicker off the mark.

'Mrs Lewis, Miss Forrest, I mean. Everyone says Bernie sings well. Would you listen to her some time, please?' Oh, Trish, that must have cost you, I thought.

'You don't have to,' said Bernadette, cool cat.

'She is good,' I put in.

'I'd love to listen to you sing.'

As we sat eating cakes behind the Great Nettle Barrier, Trish giggled.

'What's the bets that tomorrow Lord Carter will say, "Lewis, why didn't you tell me your mother was Marian Forrest? I think I'd better hear you sing again. And on the note this time, Lewis." '

9

I like going to school.
I like coming home.
It's the bit in between I can't stand.

'Come here, Lewis,' Sir said, calling me up to his desk. He brought his face close. I drew mine back.

'Tell me, er, Charles, why didn't you say that Marian Forrest was your mother?' Somewhere behind me I heard a snort, but he took no notice. I put some mental sellotape over my mouth and decided I'd see how long I could keep it there.

'I'm a fan of hers.' Silence.

'I've got nearly all her records.' Silence.

'You must be very proud of her.' Silence.

'Is she doing anything special at the moment?' I tried to keep it up, but this time I had to speak.

'I don't know.'

He sighed. 'I see you're shy. It's probably understandable. Still when you next speak to your mother tell her your teacher would count it a privilege to make her acquaintance.'

'Eh?'

He sighed again. 'Tell her your teacher would like to meet her.'

'But she's already met Mr Merchant at a parents' evening.'

There was another snort from behind me.

He turned his face away from mine, closed his eyes and

took one of his deep breaths. 'Let's try that singing once more, shall we, and this time keep on the note, Charles, if you don't mind.'

This time I sang on the note.

And from then on I was treated differently. The voice he used to me was not the one he'd used before, and he didn't speak to me in the same way he did to the rest of the class. It was all you ever needed, too squirm-making for words. How long before Cooper started jeering and singing, 'Charlie is My Darling'? To Trish Mr Carter had other things to say.

'I hold you responsible for your brother's behaviour. It's your job to see that he isn't a menace and a hindrance to others in the classroom who are trying to get on with their work. I'm told that you can handle him, so keep him under control. Why pull that face? Apparently you've always sat next to him, so what's the matter now?'

'But I always sat with my group as well. With my friends. With Charlie.'

A wolf whistle came from Brian Cooper but Sir took no notice. 'Charles must be allowed to make rapid progress and not be hindered . . .'

'I don't hinder him! I'm as bright as he is!'

'Considerably brighter,' murmured Tam in my ear.

'Quite. But he will have to achieve very high standards indeed for his new school. But since you are a very able girl and are rightly concerned about your brother's reading, on Tuesday and Thursday afternoons you will be allowed to take him and Sandra in to the resources area and teach them with material kindly provided by Mrs Lane, as she was concerned about them both. I think you'll enjoy it.'

'But I shall miss Science, my favourite lesson. For what? Baby-minding. Instead of having my lessons.'

He took one of his deep breaths. 'We all have to make sacrifices.'

'That's rubbish. People only say that when they want you to do something they don't. That's what me mum says.'

Later, as Tam and I helped her to write out three hundred lines on the need for politeness, Tam said:

'There are times, Trish, when it is wise to be silent as a lily.'

'And you can go jump in a lake with your bloomin' lily,' she snapped.

Every afternoon now ended with singing, which could have been fine with different songs and another teacher but as it was we sat, like cats on hot bricks singing 'Nymphs and Shepherds' over and over and waiting for Sir to explode. And now I was supposed to be on his side agin the rest, the OTHER musician in the room. He asked me what I thought, got me to check who was singing off the note, made lousy jokes about my perfect pitch, which no one found funny,

57

least of all me. Another week of this an' I'll be the best hated kid in Cricklepit Combined, I groaned to Trish and Tam. Cooper and Co will hang me from the playground tree. They're bigger than I am. He was the favourite of the worst teacher we've ever had, will be written on my tombstone.

One afternoon Rocket, driven nearly out of his mind with the boredom of copying out spellings while we sang 'Nymphs and Shepherds' climbed on top of one of the bookcases and tried to fly away. The bookcase was wobbly and the whole lot descended, books, Rocket and all, crash of crashes. By the time everything had been put together again, Rocket sent to Chief Sir for punishment, a note written to Mr. Moffat (and that's a waste of time, Trish pointed out, it's Mum who matters in our house), the afternoon had passed and singing time gone.

'You might've been killed,' she grumbled on the way home, 'if that bookcase had fallen on you.'

'Danger time, danger time,' warbled Rocket.

'Shut up. I don't like it. Sometimes you give me the creeps,' she cried and ran on ahead, to find her mum had been taken into hospital and all the Moffats were flapping. I waited for Bernadette to come home, as I had to take her to sing to my mother, and listened to them arguing like a rook colony.

'You'll 'ave to stay whome, our Trish,' Dad said. 'You do the work and look after 'er.' He jerked a thumb at Toyah, who sat howling and biting her grey blanket known as Bank.

'I'm not stayin' here with you lot. You can do the cooking and cleaning. Where's Chas? He'll organize it.'

'He got a job today, and he starts tomorrow. Shurrup, Toyah.' Toyah yelled even louder.

'A job? Chas? Great. Does me mum know? She'll be pleased.'

58

'I think it was that made her ill so she had to go in,' said Tarquin, grinning, he's the one I can't stand, of all the Moffats.

'It's not likely to happen in your case, is it?' snarled Trish, and burst into tears, which is so rare with Trish that they all shut up and stared. 'Nobody cares about me mum, and she's worth all the rest of you put together,' she sobbed.

'We do, we do. You can come wi' me to see 'er tonight, and she ain't really bad, our Trish. She'll be out soon and fit to go back to 'er job.'

'Oh, yeah, that's all you care about.'

'Don't you go speaking to your dad like that, Trish, it ain't right,' said her father.

'OK. But get this clear. I'm not doing the housework and looking after you lot. Tark, you're always at home anyway. Well, do something instead of lying in bed all day.'

'Not me. Woman's stuff. I'm off. Tell our Bernie to stay home.'

'What's going on?' she asked, coming in and picking up Toyah who immediately stopped howling and just bit Bank instead. Everyone informed Bernadette at the tops of their voices. She listened, settled Toyah with a biscuit, then said,

'I'm off as well. I've got to see Charlie's mum. Coming, Charlie?'

I dragged myself away, wondering just how they were going to sort it all out and how you could make it all into music. I took Bernadette inside to my mother, and myself off back to the Moffats, where Trish had had the brainwave of sending for Nan Smith, a formidable old lady, their gran, a rhinoceros in an armoured tank, to look after them. Trish was getting ready to visit the hospital.

'Charlie, I've got nothing to take in, and no money. Charlie, I hate to ask and I will, I will pay you back but . . .'

'Hang on, I'll be back.'

Dorothy had row upon row of scent bottles and talc and everything you can think of in the bathroom. I slid a couple out from the back and shot out as fast as poss. As I left I put my tongue out at Dorothy, who was gardening.

'Oh, Charlie, imagine me mum in Chanel . . .'

'Great.'

In the distance I could hear Dorothy calling me to do my practice so I made a rude sign and got told off by Trish, saying it didn't suit me, yuck. Rocket asked me to come and help him with his wings, so I did, sucks to Dorothy. And practice.

But helping Rocket's never easy. Some of his ideas are so crazy. I hadn't a clue how to fix bamboo sticks to the edges of the bin liners for extra support, and he'd also pinched some springs out of an old sofa for launching from. We struggled on but didn't really manage anything and in the end we just flopped exhausted in the shed, Rocket with yet more bruises though he's already got so many that it didn't make an awful lot of difference. After a time he rummaged behind some boxes full of ancient junk and,

'What about that, Charlie? Great, init?'

That was a sinister rubber chicken, from the Joke Shop, I guess, looking very dead, head twisted the wrong way, a vile shade of yellow with a wicked red beak. I didn't care for the look of it at all. In his other hand he held what looked like fake plastic blood.

'Where did you get that thing?'

'Tark give it me. He bought it to scare his girl-friend and he did. But she chucked him.'

'I'm not surprised. It's horrible. Scare anybody.'

'Yeh, I know. It'll shake 'im, won't it?'

'Hey. Rocket. Whatever you've got in mind, don't,' I

60

warned but he was too busy cackling to listen. In the end I gave up and went home where my mother was waiting for me.

'You were right, Charlie. She's really very good indeed. What am I going to do about her?'

'Don't ask me, Mum. I never know what to do. But, Mum . . .'

She smiled at me.

'What, Charlie?'

'I know the Moffats better than you do and I'm not sure you've the time to get mixed up with them. They can be very . . . oh, what's the word?'

'I know the one you mean. Yes, I'll remember that.'

'You see they're great, really, and you get more and more . . .'

She nodded. 'I know.'

I wanted to go on talking to her, telling her about my friends and . . . 'Have you done your practice yet? It is very important, you know.'

I felt flat and dreary. I went off to do my practice. I didn't try out any new ideas at the end. The house felt cold and grey. A scud of rain rattled on the window. Suddenly I made up my mind. I would make my mother listen to me. I would tell her about the things that mattered to me, tell her about the music I wrote, the little songs, my secret pop collection, I'd ask her for the . . . I wouldn't be secretive, I wouldn't be sly, I'd speak out and tell people things. Like Trish always did, I'd say what I felt about that new school.

'Mum, Mum,' I shouted. I hoped Dorothy had gone out. If I could get my mother on her own we could really talk . . . maybe I'd ask her about my Dad. I hadn't done that for ages.

'Here, Charlie,' called my mother from what Dorothy

calls the drawing room, the big one at the front. She stood smiling at me, looking very pink. And pretty. She's not really old, I thought – not much older than Bonfire.

'Look who's here, Charlie. And who's brought me these beautiful flowers!'

So, you're always getting beautiful flowers, what's different about these? The man with her turned round and smiled at me.

'Hello, Charles,' he said.

It was Mr Carter.

10

*Laugh and the class laughs with you but you stay in after
school alone*

We came back into the classroom after PE in the hall and
there it was, on the teacher's desk, a dead chicken lying in a
pool of blood oozing over the spelling tests placed in a neat
pile ready to be marked.

'Oo-er-oo!' screeched Sandra, above the rest of the cries,
screams, laughs and, oh no, I caught sight of Rocket's face
grinning proudly at it as if it had just won first prize in a
chicken competition. Take that grin off your face and act
surprised, I muttered to him, and he tried but the grin kept
breaking through.

'I wonder how it got here?' he asked, not a bit convincingly.

'Yes, it's mine,' he told Sandra proudly.

'What's all this then? Hurry up and settle. Don't all crowd
my desk like that. What are you doing? Oh, I see. Someone
has been exercising its tiny sense of humour.'

We melted away to our desks. Hopefully, Brian Cooper
told him it was a dead chicken in a pool of blood . . . but his
voice died away in the stony silence that had fallen. I could
see Rocket peering round, bewildered, where were the
laughs? No laughs. It was dead as a dodo, deader than
Rocket's chicken had ever been. Flatter than flat. If Sir had
ignored it, it would have been forgotten by afternoon. But
he didn't.

63

'No one goes out to play until someone has owned up.'

'You're not keeping us all in, are you, Sir?'

'Oh yes, I am, Patricia, I am. The minute the person who placed that monstrosity on my desk owns up you are free to go. Was it you?'

Red rushed all over Trish. 'No,' she stormed. 'It's not my kind of thing.'

'Was it you, Tam Lann?'

The thought of Tam placing it there was crazy. Sir made his way round the class. Break-time passed quickly as he questioned us slowly, coming at last to Rocket, and I could see he'd suspected him all along.

'It was you, wasn't it? You're the only one stupid enough to do such a thing. I've half a mind to hang it round your neck for the rest of the day and see how you like it. Your albatross. Like you're mine. Except you don't understand that, do you, Moffat? Right. The rest of you can go. You stay where you are.'

They all evaporated at incredible speed, leaving Tam and Trish and me watching as he carried the chicken and held it above Rocket's head, arms outstretched so that he seemed a giant, miles high. Rocket tried to step away from him but was caught, held. Trish broke.

'Let him go,' she shouted, rushing at Mr Carter and grabbing his arm.

'This doesn't concern you. Don't interfere. Your brother has done something stupid and must be punished.'

'You said I was responsible for him so punish me. Another set of lines.'

'No, lines won't do this time. You are going to wear this, Moffat.'

'Just a joke, just a silly joke,' she cried, shaking his arm, trying to get at the chicken. 'It doesn't matter. We played

lots of jokes on Sir and he didn't mind. He used to play some back on us.'

Mr Carter lowered the chicken and turned from Rocket.

'I'm not a circus performer. I'm not a clown. It's not my job and it's not my nature.'

'You don't have to be a clown. Miss Plum is serious and we like her. But you're unkind and unfair . . .' and she ran out of the room. Tam and I shuffled out awkwardly behind her, not looking at Mr Carter. Rocket followed, an old, tired mop.

'This has all the feeling of a day you wish didn't happen,' Tam Lann sighed, 'but Sir is wearing an air of astonishment.'

'So will Trish when she comes back. If she comes back.'

'She will. She's not the one to run away.'

And at the end of play she appeared in the doorway, eyes red, face white, and walked up to the desk.

'I'm sorry. I shouldn't have said those things.'

'Better sit down. Tell your brother jokes are best kept at home. Now, children, we are going to change the routine a little. We shall make a start on a project. I think you're ready for one now. Sandra and Moffat, you can take your usual places for this, and we are working in groups so discussion can take place providing it's sensible. We shall study Transport through the Ages . . .'

'We've already . . .' but Tam and I both kicked Trish hard this time.

'What the heck does it matter what we're doing as long as it's a change?' I growled at her, as for the first time since Mr Carter arrived there was a babble in the classroom like old times. Later we got together under the tree outside.

'Your words seem to have rung a bell with him, Trish.'

'He might improve. Rocket, don't dare climb the tree. You've got me into enough trouble.'

'He said I didn't have to try Tiny People,' put in Sandra.

'D'you mean *Little Women*?'

'Mmmm. That's it. Clever Trish.'

'Anyway,' cried Trish, 'I'm going to forget Sir Carter. How about going to dig out the cricket gear? Time we started to play. The team should be going up soon.'

It did. In Sir's absence it appeared that Mr Carter would be organizing this, for he had put up two teams, Probables versus Possibles, what'e mean by that, asked Cooper. Trish told him, so angry that even her teeth chattered. For there wasn't a single girl on it.

Back in the classroom, she stood up and said,

'Sir?'

He sighed. 'You again? I'll give you half a minute, but no more, as you waste a lot of this class's valuable time. If you're going to achieve good standards in this class then you will have to get your fingers out . . .'

Several people did. Under the desk and not in the way he meant.

'. . . Sir?' interrupted Trish, but he droned on. No, he hadn't improved.

'. . . and buckle down to your work.'

'Are you sexist?' asked Trish, like a trumpet at full blow.

He blinked, shaken.

'I beg your pardon!'

'You've put up a list of twenty-two players and not one of them is a girl! Why?'

'Why? I'll tell you why. I don't think any girl is good enough to play cricket. Now sit down and we'll get on with Maths.'

67

11

CHARLIE: *Why are you walking along with one foot on the pavement and one foot on the road?*
ROCKET: *Oh, that's funny. I thought I'd got a limp.*

It was no good. Nobody was going to answer the door. We rang the bell and we banged the knocker but nobody came. It was clear that no one was at home at Mr Merchant's house. We stood on the front path not knowing what to do. At last someone came along and spoke to us.

'No good knocking. She's gone into hospital to have her baby and he's gone with her, then he's going to stay somewhere else with friends as he still can't manage very well. No, sorry, I haven't got the address.'

We turned to go home again, Trish, Rocket and me, walking because we hadn't got enough money for the bus.

'I don't know what to do.' I don't think I'd ever heard Trish say that before. 'I counted on talking to Sir, and it wouldn't have been like last time as we have tried to give Garters a chance and he's still . . .' her voice trailed off and we walked in a dreary silence until Rocket cried, 'Look,' and there on the pavement lay a five pound note. He'd grabbed it in a jiffy. 'Let's spend it now,' he yelled.

'Oh, no, you don't,' snapped Trish. 'I think it belongs to that woman in front. I'm giving it to her.'

'No, you're not,' shouted Rocket.

'Sometimes you're a bit much, Trish,' I bellowed. But

68

she was already running ahead, calling the woman in front to stop. She turned round, of course, as Trish explained, panting, waving at Rocket, who was trying to hide the five pound note behind his back. And this woman had a face like a hatchet. I thought she'd say we'd stolen it out of her pocket as she walked along, but no. 'Good girl,' she said as Trish forced Rocket to hand over the note, pulling awful faces as he did so.

'It's wonderful to meet honest children these days,' she said, 'so I'll give you a reward.'

I hoped it was fifty pence at least, that wouldn't be bad. Rocket nodded his head up and down, shuffling his feet and waiting.

'There you are. Go and spend that.' And off she went, leaving us to peer at what was in Trish's hand. A fivepenny bit.

'No, don't hit Trish,' I said to Rocket, 'the four-eyed git can't help being barmy. Has it occurred to you, Patricia, that the note probably didn't even belong to that woman in the first place? Women like her usually carry money in their purses, not loose in their pockets. She's probably laughing her head off and here we are with fivepence. Between us. You have it, Rocket. Not much point in sharing it.'

'I'm sorry. I think you're probably right, Charlie. But my luck's right out at the moment.' Then she straightened up and her eyes began to swivel. 'But I won't give up. I'll show 'em.'

'Who?'

'Everybody,' she shouted at the top of her voice, causing a lot of people to turn round in astonishment. And at that moment a bus drew up alongside and Rocket's bus driver friend looked out.

'Jump on,' he cried.

'We've only got fivepence,' Trish called up to him.

'I'll treat you, gorgeous. And your horrible friends. Only put that one . . .' pointing at Rocket . . . 'under the seat.'

'I'll bite all the ankles, then,' he cried, grinning and running upstairs, laughing at his own joke, which caused several passengers to go downstairs for greater safety.

'He called me gorgeous. Do you think I'm pretty, Charlie?'

'No.'

'D'you think I'll be pretty when I'm older?'

'How the heck do I know? Or care. And what d'you want to be pretty for? Bernadette's pretty and she's a horrible little cow. You don't want to be like her, do you?'

'She's pretty and she sings better than me. And Toyah likes her better than me and so does my Dad.'

'Shut up. What does it matter? I don't care if I never lay eyes on her again. We've got enough to worry about with Sir Carter and his music.'

'His music. Why is it always His music? Why not Our Music? That's it! Charlie, Charlie, THAT'S IT!'

'Cool it, Trish. Everyone's glaring at us. Being out with you two is like being out with a zoo.'

'Don't be so snobby and middle-class.'

'You said you had an idea. What is it?'

'Not one idea. Two. You, Charlie, will form a group to play Our Music and I shall organize a Girls' Cricket Eleven. And beat the boys.'

We stayed outside yacking for ages, Trish firing on all cylinders. At last I went in. My mother called out to me,

'Come in, Charlie. Come and join us.'

Dorothy brayed, 'Everyone's dying to meet you.'

I went in warily. Mr Schliemann was there, and some other people, big, old, grand, far away. And among them, smiling, raising a glass to me, stood Mr Carter.

'I . . . I . . . sorry . . .'

I turned and ran up the stairs, running away, running away, and then threw up in the bog.

'Poor Charlee,' said Hortense, wiping my face gently. 'Eet was zat 'orreeble feesh we ate. Poor Charlee.'

'Yeh, the fish,' I muttered. 'It was the fish.'

12

What happens to a flea when it gets angry?
It goes hopping mad.

Next day I was sick again, so maybe it really was the fish after all. It was great to have a day away from school, which had been getting a bit much lately. I lay in bed and read in the morning, but by the afternoon I was OK, so I worked at my songs and had another go at the tree pattern, and I began to think I was getting somewhere, though nobody was gonna like it except me, not that I cared. After tea Trish and Rocket called to see how I was but couldn't stay as they'd got to go to the hospital. I felt peaceful just thinking about my music, all that really matters, and realized I was as bad as old Garters with 'My Music', and at that moment the door bell rang, and with it came an awful feeling of doom. And I was right. It was the man himself. I heard my mother's voice as the door closed behind him. I stared down at Hortense from the top of the stairs.

' 'e has brought zees grapes.'

'You 'ave 'em. They'd choke me.'

The door bell rang again. This time two men entered, one of them Mr Schliemann who nodded up and down in a moly fashion.

'I 'spec zay arrange weez your maman about ze future, no?' Hortense smiled.

'Yuck.' I felt sick again.

'Charlee, 'ave you done your practeese yet? Your propaire practeese, not zee old bangeengz and crasheengs. Dorotee, she eez so cross eef you do not do your practeese.'

And that's all anyone in this flippin' house ever says to me. Not are you all right, are you happy, is it OK, Charlie? No, no, no, no, flippin' no. All I am is an extra musical instrument round the place. HAVE YOU DONE YOUR PRACTICE?

'No, I haven't done my flaming practice. And what's more I'm not doing it with him in the house. I'm going out and when I come back I'll do my practice when I want to and what's more I'll play what I want for a change and you can all get stuffed.'

Cries of Charlee, Charlee followed me out as I stormed over to the Moffats and watched TV with them waiting for Trish to come in. Toyah, not in bed with her mother not being home, came and put her head against my arm, saying nice Charlie, which was just as well, as I don't know what I've have done if she'd given me her usual welcome. After a bit I heard Trish in the kitchen, so I went in there.

'Me mum's all right,' she began.

'Good. Listen, Trish. I've thought it all out. I know what to do, who I want in the group and what to do for the concert. We'll do it for Mr Merchant's end of term do, the fourth year show. We'll take no notice of what Garters's doing – work on our own. And, Trish, I want you to do the announcing, the organizing, give the orders, you're the boss, OK? I don't want to be on stage much – I don't like it – so I'll do lots of taping, use different tracks, I can hear it, could be good.'

'Great.'

'We'll have Tam and Alex, Sandra can sing a bit, you're

OK, Brian Cooper isn't bad, but – and you won't like this, Trish – we need Bernadette.'

'Do we have to?'

'She's the difference between Number One and Number Forty-three in the charts, or nearly.'

'She isn't fourth year.'

'Forget it, then.'

'OK OK OK. She can be in it. As long as there's something for Rocket as well.'

'Rocket shall play an instrument if I have to fix him down with super glue.'

'Charlie, what's happened to you?'

'What are you on about?'

'You're different. More alive . . .'

'Of course I'm alive, don't talk rubbish. Trish, I wish I'd got a synthesizer for this concert, that's what I'd like, to make music for today, not play somebody else's from the past . . .'

'Your mother . . .?'

'Can you imagine her face if I asked her? The mind boggles. I don't fit in my mother's world, Trish, and I can't tell her. They're all expecting me to perform like her an' all I want to do is write funny little tunes and songs about people and things. Like trees. Like you and Rocket. I wrote tunes about you two, did you know?'

'About me? Why didn't you tell me? Play it for me.'

'Yeh, I will. Some time. Listen, Trish, but don't tell anybody. My dad, my dad wrote songs. I found some shoved crumpled at the back of the piano stool and I played them and they made me feel great – different – as if I knew who I was. Not Marian Forrest's son who's never gonna be like she is because I just can't be. And I don't want to be. I'm like my dad. It's making the music that matters most. I wrote an accompaniment and backing for the songs and then I started to do some of my own. But all I get at home is practice, practice for the new school – where they'll just make me into another performer . . .'

'Well, tell your mother . . .'

'I can't. I can't talk to her . . .'

'Couldn't you write songs *and* be a concert performer? There's no law against it and it'd make your mother happy.'

'Playing great works over and over isn't for me. It means more to me to catch the melody I'm looking for than play other people's masterpieces, even if my stuff is little and unimportant. I always think I could talk to my dad and tell him this but I don't know where he is. And I know my mother would be disappointed because I think this is what he tried to do, and he failed, while she made it. So everything's worked out for me to be like her, and Bernadette would say Charlie's lucky, he's got it made . . .'

'And so you have,' Bernadette said, coming out of the shadows, for it had gone dark while we were talking, 'and you're dead lucky. And a fool. I'd know what to do if I was you, I'd grab everything going.'

She switched on the lights and I turned to leave. There'd be trouble back at home. Trish followed me out.

'That sneaky cat was listening all the time. Are you sure you want her in the group?'

'What she's like doesn't alter the fact that she can sing. Oh, and Trish . . .'

'Yes?'

'Count me in on the cricket. To help you, I mean. I'm no good at it and I'm a boy, but I'll score or somethin'. Anything to put him down.'

'I think you hate him nearly as much as I do.'

'Yeh, but you're lucky. You don't have him at your house bringing flowers for your mother.'

'Nobody's ever brought flowers for my mother, Charlie Lewis. Remember that.'

We got together under the big tree to sort out a group and a team. Trish finally got enough girls, though she had to kick Sandra into it because she didn't think her mother would like her playing cricket. Take your pick, said Trish, either your mother or me and I'm here right now, so Sandra agreed to play. Cricket would be practised in the dinner hour, and the first meeting of the group would be at my house next week when my mother and Dorothy set off on a new tour. This time I wasn't going to let Hortense keep anybody out. In the meantime I'd get music and instruments and tapes ready.

Walking home from school, 'If you told your mother she might help,' said Trish.

'More likely she'll tell Garters,' I said gloomily. 'He's always round at our house now.'

Rocket stared at me. 'You mean ... you mean ... courting?'

'I suppose you could call it that.'

'You mean he fancies her? Well, she's nice, your mum, but if she fancies him, yuck and double yuck.'

'All the time he brings her flowers. Place is full of the bloomin' things. Smelly, they are.'

'What are you going to do?'

'What can I do? He pretends he likes me. Brings me chocolates. I won't touch them. I'd rather take poison.'

'You bring 'em round to me, Charlie. I don't mind if they are his. Don't make any difference to the taste.'

My mother was to leave for Europe on Thursday and the house would seem empty again, after she'd been home for quite a while. She'd be back soon, she said, to finalize arrangements for the new school. After school on Wednesday Bernadette came in once more to sing for her, what a lovely girl she told me afterwards, so pretty and gentle. Gentle? She must be crazy, my mother, Bernadette was about as gentle as a razor blade. But then she also liked Dorothy, I supposed, and Mr Carter. She just had no judgement, my mother. Hortense? Well, she wasn't so bad these days, ever since I called her a cow, which just goes to show people are crazy.

After Bernadette had gone Dorothy began moaning and grinding on about her coming in to sing. Why was my mother overstraining herself before an important tour, bothering with all these trivial people round here, when she should be taking care of herself and her career?

'No one is unimportant, Dorothy.'

'I'm only trying to take care of you. You let people impose on you.' Dorothy worked up her voice into a shriek. 'You owe something to your public, you know. I can't go on working for you if you don't co-operate.'

'There are plenty of other people willing to work for me,' said my mother and her voice was the coldest thing I've ever heard. Dorothy rushed past Hortense and me in the hall where we'd both been listening. Oh, la la, Hortense grinned and I realized she didn't like Dorothy either. After a bit I played for my mother and she asked about a present and I almost said synthesizer, but I didn't dare, and then, and then, I realized it wasn't me she was talking about, it was Bernadette! What did I think she'd like, a pretty dress, Bernadette would look lovely in a pretty dress, wouldn't she? She, my mother, really enjoyed buying pretty dresses, I always wished you'd had a sister, Charlie. I couldn't believe my ears. Rat poison, she'd love that, I said under my breath

77

and went off to find Rocket, forgetting he'd said he was visiting his mother.

He didn't want to go, he hated hospitals, he said, so we hid till Trish and their dad had gone, though they called and called for him before they left. We were in our cleaning cupboard and no one thought of looking there. Rocket wanted to be Tarzan, so I played a big ape and we had a scrap. Next we got out the dustbinliner wings and I stuck the polythene to his wrists and back with sellotape. It wasn't very satisfactory but it would have to do. Fitting the springs on to his feet was much more difficult. In the end he climbed on the shed roof, I sat behind him and tied the springs round and round with string. He stood up, wobbling like crazy.

'Watch me fly, Charlie,' he cried and launched himself off the shed.

His screams were terrible. For an awful moment I thought he'd killed himself. What will Trish say? I thought. I scrambled down as fast as I could to where he lay on the ground, one foot twisted under in a peculiar fashion. Broken? What shall I do? Stay there, Rocket, not that he was likely to go anywhere, the state he was in, and charged off to find somebody, anybody, and it happened to be Chas. He carried Rocket inside, Rocket sobbing sadly.

'Is he broken?'

'Dunno. Twisted, I think. He'll live. Dead stupid you are, Rocket, doing yourself up like this. You can't fly. People can't. They're the wrong shape. I'll fix 'im up, Charlie, don't worry.'

Shaken, I went back home, wanting to talk to my mother for a kind of comfort, thinking I will be nice to her – even if she does like Bernadette – for she's going away in the morning, so I put my head round the music room door. And there, hand in hand on the sofa, listening to Mozart, were my mother and Garters. I gulped, banged the door shut and ran upstairs, where I put on the wildest rock at maximum volume, not caring who heard. Someone knocked on the door, and tried to open it, but it was bolted. I heard Garters call out, 'Come along, Charles. Open up. Don't be ridiculous,' but I took no notice at all, just wound the music round and round me like a defensive force field, and stayed inside it.

In the morning, she knocked on my door again. 'Please let me in, Charlie. I've got to go now.' I didn't answer.

'Charlie, goodbye. Charlie?'

'We'll miss the train. Come on. If he wants to sulk, let him,' I heard Dorothy call.

'Goodbye, Charlie. When I come back we'll have a talk. I promise.'

When I was sure she'd gone I unbolted the door.

I slipped out of the house and ran to school without Trish and Rocket, but when I got there, I felt mean remembering the ankle and Trish having to cope, so I ran back like the wind and found that Chas had got a van from somewhere and was busy getting a peevish Rocket into it. At last we got away, arriving late so that everyone was there in the class-room already with Mr Carter. So was Chief Sir, and Buggsy, and Mrs Bennet, the secretary, they were all there and they were staring—

At a notice board behind Sir's desk. On it Mr Merchant used to pin class news, and notices, and bits from the papers, and poems or jokes he'd come across. We used to pin things on it as well, photographs taken at the week-end, menus if we'd been taken out, programmes, league tables. Mr Carter uses it for our many test results, Tam always at the top, Trish second, me third, and Rocket at the bottom, just above Sandra, it doesn't change much. All these had been torn off and thrown on the floor, together with the papers off the desk. Acrylic paint had been thrown over them and splurged in bands of swirling colour. Behind the desk a window was shattered and glass lay everywhere.

They all turned to look at us croffling in with Rocket. And they stared and stared, as Trish turned red and Rocket white. You could see what they were thinking. It was written over all their faces.

'Well, Moffat, and when did you get around to doing all this?' drawled Mr Carter, Sir.

13

Why did the boy take the axe to school?
He thought it was breaking-up day.

I stood in Chief Sir's office – not a place I'd often been in. Our class had been taken to sit on the hall floor while the mess was cleaned up and we all went one by one to be questioned by Chief Sir.

'Like an interrogation by the police in a whodunnit. Or . . . or like other interrogations. I do not care for them very much,' said Tam, and his face changed into something old and sad.

'Don't worry, Trish,' I managed to say to her before we were all silenced by Sir. We were to sit on the floor absolutely still, doing nothing while we waited, though Rocket was allowed a chair once Mr Carter had asked Mrs Bennet to check that there really was something wrong with the ankle. Poor lamb, she murmured, and rubbed his mop of white hair.

We went in alphabetical order to see Chief Sir. He told me to pull up a chair and sit opposite to him on the other side of the desk, then he remained silent for a long time, fingers pointed into steeples, bushy eyebrows twitching over the famous blue eyes which were said to have X-ray vision. The Chief Sir theme tune was playing in my head. I've never yet been able to finish it, there's always a point where it comes to a halt and won't go any further, but something was there, working at the back of my mind, if I could only seize it and hang on to it. He stood up and with an old battered teapot began to water a really grisly plant on the window-sill. It looked like those horror pods in *The Invasion of the Body Snatchers*. Perhaps he intended them to take over the children, I thought. Then, still with his back to me, he spoke suddenly so that I jumped.

'Did Moffat damage himself coming through that window? And were you helping him at the time?'

'Oh, no, no, Sir. He twisted his ankle last night trying to fly – I mean jump – off the shed roof.'

'I know all about Rodney's attempts to fly. One day soon, he'll give them up, lose faith that he can do it. Then he'll

grow up and join the dole queue. Sad.' He paused for a moment and went on.

'And you didn't help him at all?'

'No, Sir.'

'Do you think Trish did it?'

'No, she might do something awful to Mr Carter but not that kind of thing.'

'That's what I thought. Do you have any idea at all who did it?'

'No, Sir.'

'You wouldn't tell me even if you had.'

There was no answer to that.

'Mr Carter likes you. You could help him a bit more. He doesn't usually teach in this type of school.'

There wasn't anything to say to that either. But I opened my mouth.

'Yes?'

'It might have been kids from outside. Like the ones who took our cassette players when I was working on something.'

'Oh, you would remember that. Yes, we are investigating that possibility. Send the next child in.'

At the door I turned round to him and said in a rush, 'Sir, I do know Rocket didn't do it.'

'Thank you, Charlie. You can go now.'

It was a most peculiar day. Everyone was restless. At last we were allowed back into the classroom. In the dinner hour everyone yacked on about vandalism but I grabbed some manuscript paper, disappeared into a corner and dotted down my Chief Sir theme which had come. Spot on. I got it down.

Rocket came and sat miserably beside me.

'Charlie, I didn't do it.'

'I know. I told Chief Sir.'

'But Carter thinks I did. He gives me nasty looks. I don't like him, Charlie. I wish he'd go.'

'Soon. He'll be going soon. Then it'll be all right again.'

But it wasn't going to be that soon. Chief Sir came in to tell us that Mr Merchant was the proud father of a baby boy to be called James, and that he'd sent a box of chocolates for the class, to celebrate with at break time. But Bonfire was not as well as she should be and he'd applied for leave, so Mr Carter would stay with us for a while longer which of course would compensate for the absence of Mr Merchant if anything could. Then he toddled off, humming the first movement from Beethoven's Seventh. What a man. Oh, you should've heard Trish on the way home.

On Saturday afternoon the kids wanting to join the group came round to my house.

'No, no, no, no,' Hortense twittered, when she opened the door to Tam, Bernadette, Sandra, Alex, Brian, Trish, Rocket and the rest.

'Hortense, belt up. If you don't let them in and keep quiet about it, I shall tell Dorothy you had your boy-friend here last night.'

Her mouth fell open, then she opened and closed it just like a goldfish.

''ow deed you know?'

'Never you mind. Now forget we're here. Except we'll need coke and crisps later. OK?'

'Shall I curtsey now or later, Mr Lewis?' asked Trish, grinning her head off.

'You can shut up as well. I'm running this end of it.'

We made a start – pretty ghastly it was – but . . . but . . . it was a start.

On Monday when we got to school all the English work books, comprehension books and the *New and Improved* . . . had been stuck together with super glue. So had Sir's book of graded spelling tests. Super glue had been splashed around very generously.

'Whatter laugh,' grinned Brian Cooper. 'Wish I'd fought of it.'

We weren't laughing quite so much when we were told that once more we were going to see Chief Sir.

I waited while he watered the body-snatching plant before he spoke.

'It's always pleasant to have a little chat with you, Charlie. You're one of the few who don't look hurt and bewildered if I use a word of more than one syllable.'

'Thank you, Sir.'

'How is your mother? Well, I trust. Probably my most remarkable pupil, though I also remember with a degree of affection the notorious bank robber who attended here. A very quietly-spoken boy he was, much like yourself. Secretive, devious. You know that word?'

'Yes, Sir.'

He swirled round and his voice was suddenly like the most rancid notes a guitar can make, setting every nerve on edge.

'What are you hiding?'

I was terrified. I'd heard about his anger, a school legend, but I'd never encountered it before. 'N-n-nothing.'

'I don't believe you. You know something, don't you? Who are you shielding?'

'Nobody,' I squeaked.

'Your friends? Patricia and Rodney. Rocket and Trish. You'd do anything for them, wouldn't you? Your only friends in the times you've been lonely?'

I nodded, trying not to cry.

'But it can't go on, you know. No one in this school is going to be victimized because of being different. Not even, Charlie Lewis, a teacher. Send in the next child.'

All day we were quiet, ghosts of children. But the following morning Mr Carter's immaculate track-suit, PE kit and training boots were found outside. It had been raining all night and they were soaked. All possible privileges were cancelled.

'Someone only has to own up,' he stated for the hundredth time and the same closed faces looked back at him. But Sandra cried. And Trish stood up.

Ignoring Sir, she cried to the class, 'Oh, come on, whoever it is, own up and let us off the hook. Stop messing about like this. It's useless taking it out on Mr Carter, because he doesn't understand us.' She swung back to him, 'You don't, you know, Sir.'

Mr Carter looked pale and tired. 'No, I don't understand you. I find you nearly all quite dreadful, if you want to know. I've tried harder than you think, Patricia, and I'm still convinced that my ways are the right ones. But perhaps we can find a compromise. If the vandal will own up and stop doing these stupid and useless things, then I'll try to find out more of your ways of doing things for the rest of my time with you.'

No one stood up. I hadn't thought they would.

But Trish said, 'Thank you, Mr Carter. There is something you could do for us if you would.'

14

Why did the Romans build straight roads?
So the Britons couldn't hide round corners.

The fourth year always had a terrific time in that last term with Mr Merchant. Last year's made an encampment in the classroom, living it up, prehistoric style, for a week. Sir got the idea from a television series, where a group of people lived in an Iron Age village for a year. That could hardly be managed at Cricklepit Combined, but they wore skins and primitive clothes and made pots and weapons and drew cave pictures, and on the last day of the week visited the famous prehistoric cavern, twenty miles away, for their school trip. We hadn't done any of this.

And that is what Trish explained to Mr Carter, who sat poker-faced before stating that creating a prehistoric environment was beyond his capabilities, even if we did already possess some of the basic requirements. Here he glanced at Rocket, and Tam smiled his first smile for days.

And so did Trish. At Mr Carter for the first time. Trish's smile is like the sun coming up all in a rush just like that, and he smiled back. Maybe it might not all have been so bad in class if she'd not taken agin him in the first place.

'Oh no, it's not the camp bit. It's the trip. You see, it was all ordered and paid for last term and now all our treats are to be taken away cos of the vandal we shan't get it and it's jolly hard on the rest who didn't do anything. And we shan't be able to go later because it gets booked up. So, if you could ask if we could be let off for that, then we'd try harder at the singing and everything for you.'

He sat in silence and thought about it while we waited. At last he spoke, 'Yes, I'll do that.' And a gasp went up for we hadn't thought he would agree, and that Trish had been pushing it, as she often does, even to ask him. 'But,' he continued, 'on condition that there's no more trouble between now and the day of the trip. And that you see that your brother behaves.'

He could've left that last bit out.

So there we were, climbing on to the coach with Miss Plum and her class, Mrs Bennet, Mrs Rowley, the helper, and half a dozen mums, Mr Carter in jeans, fall about, and Miss Plum in a tee-shirt, giggle, giggle, nudge, nudge. The sun had also arrived after days of rain, bringing warm weather. All the usual trip things, three on a seat, packed lunches, cans, gift money, cameras, radios, casual gear, piling into a seat with Trish and Rocket, ankle almost better now.

But at the last minute, a most extraordinary sight – wearing a Sherlock Holmes hat, a suit patterned like a chessboard, huge wellies, and carrying a walking stick – Chief Sir arrived and climbed on to the coach! But he never went on school trips. Never!

'Carry on as if I weren't here,' he announced from the doorway so utter silence fell but as we drove off into the bright morning, mums waving us off, someone started to sing and we were well away. Miss Plum stopped the sweet-eaters, cleared up after Brian Cooper who was sick, and it was just like always, deafening noise, a bumpy ride. As we climbed out, the heat hit us.

'Gift shop first, then you might be able to pay some attention to the cavern,' Miss Plum announced, being in charge. The two classes surged forward, taking the three assistants along with them.

'I'd never have believed it,' I heard Mr Carter say, 'it's like a zoo.'

'They'll calm down,' Chief Sir replied.

I bought Hortense a scarf and a guide book. I didn't feel like buying anything for my mother. Everyone gave her things. Remembering that, I went back to the counter and brought a sprig of lucky heather set in a brooch for Mrs Moffat. I hoped she'd like it. Rocket had bought her something as well.

'D'you like it, Charlie?'

'But it's a dog collar. You haven't got a dog.'

'No, but me mum will love it. Good, init?'

At last the noise quietened down to the dark red silence of the cave, where the guides took over from the teachers and organized us into single files and orderliness. I stood beside Tam, separated from Trish and Rocket. Our guide droned on in his special voice, 'One hundred thousand years ago the caves were used for shelter by prehistoric man. They were the first visitors ... In the history of mankind the records of this cavern go further back than any other cave . . .' We stared at coloured stalagmites and stalactites, at the marks on the wall, the tooth of a sabre-tooth tiger, and a theme softly crawled up into my head and walked lightly into my brain, causing the hairs to prickle all down my back, and for once I didn't want it – any more than I want the old mad monster one – and I tried to shake it away, push it down. All I wanted to do today was to gaze at this strange and alien place where people had lived and died. People like Rocket, maybe, no, not like Rocket, they'd have had to be like Trish to survive, or they'd all have perished from cold or hunger or disease

89

or wild animals and there'd be no us . . . no us . . . no us.

I wished Sir had been with us. He'd have brought it all to life better than anyone, brought the men and women from the past into the present, now, made everything real, whereas more and more strongly I felt that everything around me could vanish in a moment, the children, the guides, Chief Sir and Miss Plum, Mr Carter and the mums, leaving only the great cave . . . and the hairs rose on my spine again and the cave melody played in my head, stronger now, sure of itself, taking me over . . .

'Rocket's gone,' whispered Trish in my ear, slipping in beside me.

'He can't be.'

'Well, he is.'

The long string of children looked at the guide and listened in the semi-gloom.

'I've made my way all along and he isn't with us,' whispered Trish.

'Please don't talk while I'm speaking,' said the guide.

Quietly, as the kids pushed forward to get a good view of the spectacular grotto now coming into sight, Trish and I stepped back and back till they had moved beyond us and we were alone. I remembered seeing a narrower passage off to the right further back, not part of the main route followed by visitors. Now out of sight of everybody we ran back and into it, the music in my head playing fortissimo, demanding me to take notice of it, listen, look at me, look at me, look at me . . . The passage turned, sloped rapidly and came to a dead end, blocked at some time by a fall. There was no Rocket. We ran back into the main cave and back again to a passage on the left, very narrow and low, with a notice saying, NO ENTRY. DANGER.

We ran into it as the music screamed terror. The path

branched into two, getting darker as we went further from the main path.

'Which?' I asked.

'We'll take the right first,' Trish said, and on we went until ahead of us loomed absolute blackness. We stopped.

'I can't go on.'

'I've got to find him,' said Trish and she stepped forward, arms outstretched, and called 'Rocket! Rocket!' The cave re-echoed all around us, 'Rocket . . . Rocket . . . Rocket . . . Rocket . . .' as its theme roared through my head like the tide pounding up and down on the shore.

'Come back or we're lost, too . . . Trish . . . Trish . . .' Trish . . . Trish . . . Trishhhh . . . the echoes sounded on and on all around us.

And she came back. 'Let's fetch Chief Sir. Let's go back to them . . .' Them . . . them . . . them . . . them . . .

'Just the left-hand side and then we go back . . . back . . . back . . .'

This one grew wider as it darkened, though not too dark to see Rocket, crouched against the side of the cave, head turned to the wall. We ran to him.

'Come on, old chap, come,' but he wouldn't stir.

'Poor Rocket,' he whispered, and the cave whispered with him eerily, 'Rocket . . . Rocket . . . Rocket . . .'

'Trish, you'll have to get them. I'll stay here.'

She left like the wind, and I sat down beside him, while the music, triumphant now, thundered and surged in my head, bringing with it the long darkness of the cold nights, the wild hunting, the flames of the cave fires, and strange faces that came nearer and nearer till I put my arms round Rocket and buried my face in his shaggy hair, while the sounds washed over and round me, drowning me.

Chief Sir pulled me to my feet as Mr Carter lifted up Rocket.

'You should have checked them in advance,' grumbled the guide. 'We do get them like this, but not usually two at a time.'

'N-n-nothing wrong with me,' I muttered. 'It's Rocket. He's got cl-cl-claustrophobia.'

'You've caused a disturbance,' went on the guide, who seemed to have taken a particular dislike to Mr Carter. 'Sometimes I think you teachers just can't be bothered. This lad needs special care.' He pointed at Rocket hanging limply, held by Mr Carter. 'As for you, you young monkey, you shouldn't be running about everywhere. Girls ought to know better.' He and Trish glared at each other.

'You're unfair,' complained Mr Carter. 'I've done my best with this trip. And if you want to know, this boy, Moffat, has caused me nothing but trouble from my first day. Yes, he needs care all right; he causes chaos, disruption, vandalism and now this.'

92

We made our way along towards the entrance, the cavern getting wider, the roof higher as we walked, and occupied as they were with Rocket I hoped they couldn't see how strange I felt trying to reach daylight. For now the music had almost taken over completely, cutting me off from everything else, leaving nothing of me as we went along, only sound, sound, sound, sound, sound . . . I couldn't bear it. I had to stop it.

'But Rocket wasn't the vandal,' I said, my voice out of control, slipping and sliding, then soaring high as it fought with the cavern theme joining the mad monsters in my head. 'You know he couldn't have done it – his ankle – and then he's too nice – always trying to be good – it couldn't be him – it had to be – someone – sly. Sly – like you said, Trish. It had to be me. Even the chicken, Mr Carter.'

The music slowed its terrible tempo, and a sweeter melody was plucked out of the air, calming, gentle. Just ahead was the entrance.

Somewhere near, yet far away, Chief Sir sighed a deep sigh.

'Charlie, I thought you'd never come out with it.'

Outside the cave the sun shone down warmly.

15

The school band should be banned.

Mr Carter left at last. Mr Merchant came back and the end of term arrived.

'Children, you have now reached the moment you've all been waiting for – no, not the moment when we all go home for the Summer holidays – but finishing-up time,' said Mr Merchant. We could hear him quite clearly from where we sat behind the stage curtains. 'For here is the fourth year with a concert to send you on your way rejoicing. As you know, this offering is usually arranged by me, but since I've been conspicuous by my absence for most of this term, Trish Moffat is in control. She's much better at organizing than I am, by the way, so let's welcome her, the fourth year and Charlie's Rockets.'

It seemed that millions of hands clapped as we trembled, then the curtains were drawn back, and there sat the school in front of us in the school hall, darkened though it was afternoon, lit by coloured lights, a mirror ball and pin spots, and behind us the back cloth we'd made with spray and stencils, the stars and planets, Saturn with its rings, shining silver. Trish came on in pink satin, her hair floating and flaming. The fourth year, those not controlling curtains, props and lights, sat on cushions round the edge and back of the stage, and in the centre, Trish and Sandra, Alex on guitar, Tam the piano, Julia the drums, to the right, Rocket with the big cymbal, and to the far right, but next to him, where I could kick him if necessary, me with tapes and tracks. Chimes, bells, tambourines and recorders had been distributed around, a piccolo, a tin whistle and a mouth organ, the lot.

We'd agreed to start with songs all the school would know, even the little ones, so we launched off with Trish and Sandra, the group warming themselves up as I knew we'd be grisly at first, singing 'Yellow Bird', 'Bright Eyes', 'Lord of the Dance', 'Morning Has Broken', 'Fame', 'Lily the Pink', and 'All Around my Hat I Wear a Green Willow'. The playing was terrible, but it didn't matter, as the school was singing so loud you couldn't hear much anyway, and it gave people time to stop feeling so nervous.

I felt almost laid back by now, so I looked to see if I could spot anyone in the lighting, and there – oh no – I unlaid back very quickly because sitting beside Chief Sir, centre middle, was, I felt sure, Mr Carter, oh lord, still it was too late now, he'd just have to put up with it. And there was an empty chair, I thought, on the other side of Chief Sir, not fair, we weren't supposed to have guests to this concert, which was always for school only, the fourth years' good-bye.

And the school was enjoying it, yelling their heads off, and I nudged Rocket, who slowly and ever so carefully, as I'd shown him how a hundred times, started to bang his cymbals, quietly at first, then crescendoing and reverberating as loud as thunder, till the music died down, and the coloured lights went out, the white and silver lights came on, and I put on my first tape, extracts from Holst's *Planet Suite*, 'Jupiter, the bringer of Jollity', and 'Mars, the Bringer of War', that most frightening of music, almost as bad as my mad monsters. And now for me, for all of us, this was nearly

95

as terrifying as the music as Rocket moved from his cymbal to the centre of the stage, the group alone began Police's 'Walking on the Moon', while Rocket in a white suit covered with silver stars did his extraordinary walk-dance-jump in the tiny amount of room left on the stage. For we had discovered that Rocket could change his usual mad movements into a kind of mime, that went perfectly with the space music. Twice he'd fallen off the stage in rehearsal, and we nearly packed the whole space idea in when he tripped on Tam and almost knocked out Alex. It's as good as flying, he cried, so we kept on with it, especially as he looked, with his whitened face and wild hair, like nothing ever seen on this planet. Next he was the Starman waiting in the sky, who'd like to come and meet us but he thinks he'd blow our minds, too true, Sir had said when he watched him at rehearsal. Then at last, he sat down safely by his cymbal and we breathed again. And Alex and I sang Bowie's 'Space Oddity', with Alex as Ground Control and me singing one of my favourite characters, Major Tom, floating in his tin can far above the moon, watching the blue planet earth. We used everyone, all the sounds we could raise from all the instruments, a four-track tape and hand-clapping. I felt great. And it was over too soon.

And a rest with 'Pass the Dutchie on the Left-hand Side', 'Mull of Kintyre' and then, Sandra and Trish was 'Ragged Coat'.

'And now,' Trish said, 'it's Puzzle Time. Charlie will play a tune, and you will guess who or what it is when the music stops. I don't mean "Danny Boy" or "Humpty Dumpty", I mean Something or Somebody at our School.'

This was a gamble. It worked fine when we first tried it on our fourth year, but then they knew me. What the others would make of it we couldn't be sure. If it didn't work we'd

move on to something else. I went to the piano to take Tam's place, looked at the audience, and saw my mother being taken by Mr Merchant to the empty seat by Chief Sir. Oh no, I thought she was in London. I sat down and hit the keys all wrong. For a minute, panic stations, run for the shadows, but no, there's really only one thing to do when you hit the wrong note and that's hit the right one and carry on. So I played the sounds of feet walking into the hall, whispers, a hymn tune, and a prayer. 'Assembly,' the kids roared, and breathe again, I thought, starting 'Match of the Day,' running up the pitch, a goal being scored, and 'Football,' they yelled. One of my favourites, Chief Sir, followed, easy one that, then Mr Merchant, Bugsie, Miss Plum, they got them all. Last of all, I took Rocket, and they roared his name, till he stood up and made a little bow, don't knock anything over, I prayed.

'Two more oddities,' Trish said. 'One is Charlie's tree tune, which when he first played it, sounded like the most horrible rubbish you'd ever heard in all your life. But he made us listen to it at every rehearsal and now we all think it's great. You can hear it now and we don't expect you to like it yet. But you will later. The other I won't say anything about. It speaks for itself.'

I didn't expect the kids to like my tree tune. And I found I was playing it for my mother, who'd never heard it, I wanted her to like it, to know what it was all about, what I was all about. The applause was kind and polite, school doing the right thing. I didn't look at anyone, but moved to the next.

Then I stood up suddenly. 'It's "Nimps and Sheriffs",' I said, using Rocket's name for it. The group joined in and we threw 'Nimps and Sheriffs' up in the air, then down on the floor and danced on it, turned it upside down and inside out, jazzed it up, rocked it, played ragtime with it, funk, punk, and disco, and put it to sleep. The applause this time was stupendous. And again, I didn't look at the audience, Mr Carter.

'And now, Top of the Pops,' said Trish, and we played not for the grown-ups but for the children, ending with our own Trish Trash Disco Dance, with feet stamping and hands clapping all over the hall.

And it was almost the end now. All those hours of work going so fast. We'd had the coloured lights and mirror ball for the pop music, but now, as the noise died down, the lights changed back to white and silver as Alex played reggae, 'Running Away, Running Away'. They were still clapping as Bernadette walked on.

Trish had meant to say that Bernadette was a guest singer, for as she wasn't fourth year she shouldn't have been taking part in our concert, but in the end she didn't say anything, for it seemed as natural for Bernadette to be there in the centre of the stage as for the sky to be above and the earth below. She wore a white dress and Trish had plaited her hair into hundreds and thousands with silver ribbon. I gave her the note – which she didn't need anyway – and she stood there, unmoving, totally calm, singing like a bird, with no accompaniment at all. She began with 'Sheep May Safely Graze' and when she'd finished there was a pause before they clapped, then they went wild. I always listen for that pause now. Then with no change of expression but with complete contrast she went straight into Blondie's 'Heart of Glass', and as she sang I could hear the old tales of magic and dark mountains, mysterious forests and secret towers in strange lands.

She wanted to choose her own last song – we'd agreed on the others together – and had told no one what it was. It surprised me, being so unlike the cool cat, a gentle, sad little song. 'Till the white rose blooms again, You must leave me, leave me lonely . . .'

It was only afterwards I thought she might have done it on purpose . . .

For look out, Trish, I thought, you won't be able to take it, not with the hymn afterwards, as well. We'd worked out that Bernadette should go from her last song to 'Lord Dismiss us with thy Blessing', the year's ending hymn that we always sing on the last day.

And so we did. As soon as Bernadette had finished and bowed once, the lights went on, we stood up and started to sing. But just as I'd feared when I'd heard Bernadette's tear-jerker, all these words proved too much for Trish. As we came to 'Those returning, those returning . . .', an anguished sob was heard and Trish ran down the stage steps and threw herself weeping upon the astonished form of Mr Merchant, Sir.

16

Doctor, doctor, I feel like a sheet of music.
I must make some notes for this.

And here I sit at the window waiting for my dad to arrive any minute now. My mother has driven to the airport to meet him. Trish is reading in the corner and says she will push off when he comes. She's there in case I panic and also she's nosy about him but won't admit it. And I'm scared. But I'd better go back to all that happened after the cave, as much as I can remember. Some of it blurs a bit, I'm so nervous.

After the school trip Chief Sir phoned my mother and said he thought she should come home, she told me when she got back, worried stiff, having cancelled her tour for the first time ever, which made Dorothy resign, a good thing since they hadn't got on for some time. Chief Sir had told her, she said to me, that a conversation with her son might be a good idea, but it wasn't easy as we were out of practice, but we did settle the main thing worrying me, no, she wasn't going to marry Garters, for one thing she and my father had never divorced, he'd just upped and left one day, very quietly, and for another she didn't fancy marrying him. They'd just both been lonely, she said. She'd grown to detest Dorothy and he'd worried about his teaching, with you monsters.

'But we're not monsters!'

'Oh no?'

Besides, she went on, with her life-style; galloping all over the place, marriage wasn't easy, or looking after children either, she sighed, and she appeared to have messed up both.

'But what about Dad?' I asked, stomach churning.

'He's doing well in Australia. I thought you knew. I'm going to write to him to visit us so we can sort out your future together, for it's too much for me on my own.'

'Try letting me in on it.'

'Oh yes, yes, Charlie. I didn't understand what you were like before. And you didn't help, did you? You didn't say anything. Just like your father . . .'

'Why doesn't he come and live with us again?'

She gave me a funny look. 'I'm not sure I want him even if you do, and I don't suppose he will want to give up his own life down under. You can't tie people up in neat parcels with tidy bows, Charlie. But he will – whatever we all do – keep in touch with us in future. He thought we'd just forgotten him or didn't care. Stupid, just like you, Charlie. Fancy you going in for vandalism! Edward, that's Mr Carter to you, said you were the last person he suspected.'

Mr Carter also said before he left that Trish's all-girl team could play the boys. If this was a story the girls would've won but actually the boys did, with Alex scoring fifty-three. Trish got twenty. But she wasn't put down. Wait till next time, she bawled, waving her bat. But there wasn't a next time, for a week later Mr Merchant came back and the team he put on the board included Trish and two other girls.

On Mr Carter's last Friday we held a mini concert and sang 'Nymphs and Shepherds' for him. Then Trish presented him with a potted plant and a book of poetry. (Tam suggested poetry would be good for him.) He looked shaken.

'I didn't expect this from you. I'm overwhelmed.'

'Don't be. We do it for everyone. It's one of our school traditions.'

'I'll remember this school. And especially you, Patricia.'

And so went Mr Carter. And so Sir came back and life was normal again or as near normal as possible with Sir trying to get done all we hadn't. Mr Carter came one evening to say goodbye to my mother before he went to his great Cathedral School for his new post. Trish wouldn't let me stay in, she hauled me away to look at the Merchant baby, hideous, looking like Popeye, without his pipe. She said it was beautiful. Crazy. She also said that she would like to have Sir around all the time, cos he was Sir, but she'd like Garters now and then to have a row with, as it was exciting. Like I told you, crazy.

You don't think the end of term will ever come, and then it's there and things are different for ever. My mother finished the tour she'd cut short, then came home ready to meet my father flying from Australia. There are ideas flying around as well – such as my mother doing an Australian tour – of my going back with my father for a long visit, down under – of Bernadette taking my place at the music school, through scholarships and a fund. She doesn't care, anyway. She'll make it to the top whatever, she says. My mother thinks she's wonderful. Trish won't speak about my going away. So there aren't neat bows, but a lot of knots instead. Rocket's great, though. He's determined to get on the plane with me. He's collecting hundreds of pictures of planes.

Is that the car arriving at last? It's got to be, got to be. I've been waiting for ages. No, it's gone past. I don't think he's coming. I think he changed his mind in Australia and never got on that plane, because he doesn't really care about us, doesn't care about me, and decided not to come. Waiting's awful. One of the worst ever things. But how would a waiting tune go, I wonder? Like this? And a melody prickles at the back of my neck and tingles slowly up into my head . . . that's it . . . that jingle, jangle, drag, drag . . . that's how it would be . . . that's it. I've got it. Could be good. A name. It needs a name. 'Waiting for'? 'Waiting for Tomorrow?' That's it.

'I've got a super joke,' Trish comes out with suddenly.

'Oh no, not again.'

'Yeh. Listen, Charlie. Cut Education costs. Shoot the teachers.'

'But we've had that one already!'

A car sweeps in at the gate. My mother's. And there's someone with her. The waiting melody crescendoes into a mad finale as I run to open the door.